A Sharp Frost

Tales and Poems for Winter

A Modern Odyssey Book

Silver Filigree

By Elinor Wylie

The icicles wreathing
   On trees in festoon
Swing, swayed to our breathing:
   They're made of the moon.

She's a pale, waxen taper;
   And these seem to drip
Transparent as paper
   From the flame of her tip.

Molten, smoking a little,
   Into crystal they pass;
Falling, freezing, to brittle
   And delicate glass.

Each a sharp-pointed flower,
   Each a brief stalactite
Which hangs for an hour
   In the blue cave of night.

The Snow Queen

By Hans Christian Andersen

Which Treats of a Mirror and of the Splinters

Now then, let us begin. When we are at the end of the story, we shall know more than we know now: but to begin.

Once upon a time there was a wicked sprite, indeed he was the most mischievous of all sprites. One day he was in a very good humor, for he had made a mirror with the power of causing all that was good and beautiful when it was reflected therein, to look poor and mean; but that which was good-for-nothing and looked ugly was shown magnified and increased in ugliness. In this mirror the most beautiful landscapes looked like boiled spinach, and the best persons were turned into frights, or appeared to stand on their heads; their faces were so distorted that they were not to be recognised; and if anyone had a mole, you might be sure that it would be magnified and spread over both nose and mouth.

"That's glorious fun!" said the sprite. If a good thought passed through a man's mind, then a grin was seen in the mirror, and the sprite laughed heartily at his clever discovery. All the little sprites who went to his school—for he kept a sprite school—told each other that a miracle had happened; and that now only, as they thought, it would be possible to see how the world really looked. They ran about with the mirror; and at last there was not a land or a person who was not represented distorted in the mirror. So then they thought they would fly up to the sky, and have a joke there. The higher they flew with the mirror, the more terribly it grinned: they could hardly hold it fast. Higher and higher still they flew, nearer and nearer to the stars, when suddenly the mirror shook so terribly with grinning, that it flew out of their hands and fell to the earth, where it was dashed in a hundred million and more pieces. And now it worked much more evil than before; for some of these pieces were hardly so large as a grain of sand, and they flew about in the wide world, and when they got into people's eyes, there they stayed; and then people saw everything perverted, or only had an eye for that which was evil. This happened because the very smallest bit had the same power which the whole mirror had possessed. Some persons even got a splinter in their heart, and then it made one shudder, for their heart became like a lump of ice. Some of the broken pieces were so large that they were used for windowpanes, through which one could not see one's friends. Other pieces were put in spectacles; and that was a sad affair when people put on their glasses to see well and rightly. Then the wicked sprite laughed till he almost choked, for all this tickled his fancy. The fine splinters still flew about in the air: and now we shall hear what happened next.

A Little Boy and a Little Girl

In a large town, where there are so many houses, and so many people, that there is no roof left for everybody to have a little garden; and where, on this account, most persons are obliged to content themselves with flowers in pots; there lived two little children, who had a garden somewhat larger than a flower-pot. They were not brother and sister; but they cared for each other as much as if they were. Their parents lived exactly opposite. They inhabited two garrets; and where the roof of the one house joined that of the other, and the gutter ran along the extreme end of it, there was to each house a small window: one needed only to step over the gutter to get from one window to the other.

The children's parents had large wooden boxes there, in which vegetables for the kitchen were planted, and little rosetrees besides: there was a rose in each box, and they grew splendidly. They now thought of placing the boxes across the gutter, so that they nearly reached from one window to the other, and looked just like two walls of flowers. The tendrils of the peas hung down over the boxes; and the rose-trees shot up long branches, twined round the windows, and then bent towards each other: it was almost like a triumphant arch of foliage and flowers. The boxes were very high, and the children knew that they must not creep over them; so they often obtained permission to get out of the windows to each other, and to sit on their little stools among the roses, where they could play delightfully. In winter there was an end of this pleasure. The windows were often frozen over; but then they heated copper farthings on the stove, and laid the hot farthing on the windowpane, and then they had a capital peep-hole, quite nicely rounded; and out of each peeped a gentle friendly eye—it was the little boy and the little girl who were looking out. His name was Kay, hers was Gerda. In summer, with one jump, they could get to each other; but in winter they were obliged first to go down the long stairs, and then up the long stairs again: and out-of-doors there was quite a snow-storm.

"It is the white bees that are swarming," said Kay's old grandmother.

"Do the white bees choose a queen?" asked the little boy; for he knew that the honey-bees always have one.

"Yes," said the grandmother, "she flies where the swarm hangs in the thickest clusters. She is the largest of all; and she can never remain quietly on the earth, but goes up again into the black clouds. Many a winter's night she flies through the streets of the town, and peeps in at the windows; and they then freeze in so wondrous a manner that they look like flowers."

"Yes, I have seen it," said both the children; and so they knew that it was true.

"Can the Snow Queen come in?" said the little girl.

"Only let her come in!" said the little boy. "Then I'd put her on the stove, and she'd melt."

And then his grandmother patted his head and told him other stories.

In the evening, when little Kay was at home, and half undressed, he climbed up on the chair by the window, and peeped out of the little hole. A few snow-flakes were falling, and one, the largest of all, remained lying on the edge of a flower-pot.

The flake of snow grew larger and larger; and at last it was like a young lady, dressed in the finest white gauze, made of a million little flakes like stars. She was so beautiful and delicate, but she was of ice, of dazzling, sparkling ice; yet she lived; her eyes gazed fixedly, like two stars; but there was neither quiet nor repose in them. She nodded towards the window, and beckoned with her hand. The little boy was frightened, and jumped down from the chair; it seemed to him as if, at the same moment, a large bird flew past the window.

The next day it was a sharp frost—and then the spring came; the sun shone, the green leaves appeared, the swallows built their nests, the windows were opened, and the little children again sat in their pretty garden, high up on the leads at the top of the house.

That summer the roses flowered in unwonted beauty. The little girl had learned a hymn, in which there was something about roses; and then she thought of her own flowers; and she sang the verse to the little boy, who then sang it with her:

"The rose in the valley is blooming so sweet,
And angels descend there the children to greet."

And the children held each other by the hand, kissed the roses, looked up at the clear sunshine, and spoke as though they really saw angels there. What lovely summer-days those were! How delightful to be out in the air, near the fresh rose-bushes, that seem as if they would never finish blossoming!

Kay and Gerda looked at the picture-book full of beasts and of birds; and it was then—the clock in the church-tower was just striking five—that Kay said, "Oh! I feel such a sharp pain in my heart; and now something has got into my eye!"

The little girl put her arms around his neck. He winked his eyes; now there was nothing to be seen.

"I think it is out now," said he; but it was not. It was just one of those pieces of glass from the magic mirror that had got into his eye; and poor Kay had got another piece right in his heart. It will soon become like ice. It did not hurt any longer, but there it was.

"What are you crying for?" asked he. "You look so ugly! There's nothing the matter with me. Ah," said he at once, "that rose is cankered! And look, this one is quite crooked! After all, these roses are very ugly! They are just like the box they are planted in!" And then he gave the box a good kick with his foot, and pulled both the roses up.

"What are you doing?" cried the little girl; and as he perceived her fright, he pulled up another rose, got in at the window, and hastened off from dear little Gerda.

Afterwards, when she brought her picture-book, he asked, "What horrid beasts have you there?" And if his grandmother told them stories, he always interrupted her; besides, if he could manage it, he would get behind her, put on her spectacles, and imitate her way of speaking; he copied all her ways, and then everybody laughed at him. He was soon able to imitate the gait and manner of everyone in the street. Everything that was peculiar and displeasing in them—that Kay knew how to imitate: and at such times all the people said, "The boy is certainly very clever!" But it was the glass he had got in his eye; the glass that was sticking in his heart, which made him tease even little Gerda, whose whole soul was devoted to him.

His games now were quite different to what they had formerly been, they were so very knowing. One winter's day, when the flakes of snow were flying about, he spread the skirts of his blue coat, and caught the snow as it fell.

"Look through this glass, Gerda," said he. And every flake seemed larger, and appeared like a magnificent flower, or beautiful star; it was splendid to look at!

"Look, how clever!" said Kay. "That's much more interesting than real flowers! They are as exact as possible; there is not a fault in them, if they did not melt!"

It was not long after this, that Kay came one day with large gloves on, and his little sledge at his back, and bawled right into Gerda's ears, "I have permission to go out into the square where the others are playing"; and off he was in a moment.

There, in the market-place, some of the boldest of the boys used to tie their sledges to the carts as they passed by, and so they were pulled along, and got a good ride. It was so capital! Just as they were in the very height of their amusement, a large sledge passed by: it was painted quite white, and there was someone in it wrapped up in a rough white mantle of fur, with a rough white fur cap on his head. The sledge drove round the square twice, and Kay tied on his sledge as quickly as he could, and off he drove with it. On they went quicker and quicker into the next street; and the person who drove turned round to Kay, and nodded to him in a friendly manner, just as if they knew each other. Every time he was going to untie his sledge, the person nodded to him, and then Kay sat quiet; and so on they went till they came outside the gates of the town. Then the snow began to fall so thickly that the little boy could not see an arm's length before him, but still on he went: when suddenly he let go the string he held in his hand in order to get loose from the sledge, but it was of no use; still the little vehicle rushed on with the quickness of the wind. He then cried as loud as he could, but no one heard him; the snow drifted and the sledge flew on, and sometimes it gave a jerk as though they were driving over hedges and ditches. He was quite frightened, and he tried to repeat the Lord's Prayer; but all he could do, he was only able to remember the multiplication table.

The snow-flakes grew larger and larger, till at last they looked just like great white fowls. Suddenly they flew on one side; the large sledge stopped, and the person who drove rose up. It was a lady; her cloak and cap were of snow. She was tall and of slender figure, and of a dazzling whiteness. It was the Snow Queen.

"We have travelled fast," said she; "but it is freezingly cold. Come under my bearskin." And she put him in the sledge beside her, wrapped the fur round him, and he felt as though he were sinking in a snow-wreath.

"Are you still cold?" asked she; and then she kissed his forehead. Ah! it was colder than ice; it penetrated to his very heart, which was already almost a frozen lump; it seemed to him as if he were about to die—but a moment more and it was quite congenial to him, and he did not remark the cold that was around him.

"My sledge! Do not forget my sledge!" It was the first thing he thought of. It was there tied to one of the white chickens, who flew along with it on his back behind the large sledge. The Snow Queen kissed Kay once more, and then he forgot little Gerda, grandmother, and all whom he had left at his home.

"Now you will have no more kisses," said she, "or else I should kiss you to death!"

Kay looked at her. She was very beautiful; a more clever, or a more lovely countenance he could not fancy to himself; and she no longer appeared of ice as before, when she sat outside the window, and beckoned to him; in his eyes she was perfect, he did not fear her at all, and told her that he could calculate in his head and with fractions, even; that he knew the number of square miles there were in the different countries, and how many inhabitants they contained; and she smiled while he spoke.

It then seemed to him as if what he knew was not enough, and he looked upwards in the large huge empty space above him, and on she flew with him; flew high over the black clouds, while the storm moaned and whistled as though it were singing some old tune. On they flew over woods and lakes, over seas, and many lands; and beneath them the chilling storm rushed fast, the wolves howled, the snow crackled; above them flew large screaming crows, but higher up appeared the moon, quite large and bright; and it was on it that Kay gazed during the long long winter's night; while by day he slept at the feet of the Snow Queen.

Of the Flower-Garden At the Old Woman's Who Understood Witchcraft

But what became of little Gerda when Kay did not return? Where could he be? Nobody knew; nobody could give any intelligence. All the boys knew was, that they had seen him tie his sledge to another large and splendid one, which drove down the street and out of the town. Nobody knew where he was; many sad tears were shed, and little Gerda wept long and bitterly; at last she said he must be dead; that he had been drowned in the river which flowed close to the town. Oh! those were very long and dismal winter evenings!

At last spring came, with its warm sunshine.

"Kay is dead and gone!" said little Gerda.

"That I don't believe," said the Sunshine.

"Kay is dead and gone!" said she to the Swallows.

"That I don't believe," said they: and at last little Gerda did not think so any longer either.

"I'll put on my red shoes," said she, one morning; "Kay has never seen them, and then I'll go down to the river and ask there."

It was quite early; she kissed her old grandmother, who was still asleep, put on her red shoes, and went alone to the river.

"Is it true that you have taken my little playfellow? I will make you a present of my red shoes, if you will give him back to me."

And, as it seemed to her, the blue waves nodded in a strange manner; then she took off her red shoes, the most precious things she possessed, and threw them both into the river. But they fell close to the bank, and the little waves bore them immediately to land; it was as if the stream would not take what was dearest to her; for in reality it had not got little Kay; but Gerda thought that she had not thrown the shoes out far enough, so she clambered into a boat which lay among the rushes, went to the farthest end, and threw out the shoes. But the boat was not fastened, and the motion which she occasioned, made it drift from the shore. She observed this, and hastened to get back; but before she could do so, the boat was more than a yard from the land, and was gliding quickly onward.

Little Gerda was very frightened, and began to cry; but no one heard her except the sparrows, and they could not carry her to land; but they flew along the bank, and sang as if to comfort her, "Here we are! Here we are!" The boat drifted with the stream, little Gerda sat quite still without shoes, for they were swimming behind the boat, but she could not reach them, because the boat went much faster than they did.

The banks on both sides were beautiful; lovely flowers, venerable trees, and slopes with sheep and cows, but not a human being was to be seen.

"Perhaps the river will carry me to little Kay," said she; and then she grew less sad. She rose, and looked for many hours at the beautiful green banks. Presently she sailed by a large cherry-orchard, where was a little cottage with curious red and blue windows; it was thatched, and before it two wooden soldiers stood sentry, and presented arms when anyone went past.

Gerda called to them, for she thought they were alive; but they, of course, did not answer. She came close to them, for the stream drifted the boat quite near the land.

Gerda called still louder, and an old woman then came out of the cottage, leaning upon a crooked stick. She had a large broad-brimmed hat on, painted with the most splendid flowers.

"Poor little child!" said the old woman. "How did you get upon the large rapid river, to be driven about so in the wide world!" And then the old woman went into the water, caught hold of the boat with her crooked stick, drew it to the bank, and lifted little Gerda out.

And Gerda was so glad to be on dry land again; but she was rather afraid of the strange old woman.

"But come and tell me who you are, and how you came here," said she.

And Gerda told her all; and the old woman shook her head and said, "A-hem! a-hem!" and when Gerda had told her everything, and asked her if she had not seen little Kay, the woman answered that he had not passed there, but he no doubt would come; and she told her not to be cast down, but taste her cherries, and look at her flowers, which were finer than any in a picture-book, each of which could tell a whole story. She then took Gerda by the hand, led her into the little cottage, and locked the door.

The windows were very high up; the glass was red, blue, and green, and the sunlight shone through quite wondrously in all sorts of colors. On the table stood the most exquisite cherries, and Gerda ate as many as she chose, for she had permission to do so. While she was eating, the old woman combed her hair with a golden comb, and her hair curled and shone with a lovely golden color around that sweet little face, which was so round and so like a rose.

"I have often longed for such a dear little girl," said the old woman. "Now you shall see how well we agree together"; and while she combed little Gerda's hair, the child forgot her foster-brother Kay more and more, for the old woman understood magic; but she was no evil being, she only practised witchcraft a little for her own private amusement, and now she wanted very much to keep little Gerda. She therefore went out in the garden, stretched out her crooked stick towards the rose-bushes, which, beautifully as they were blowing, all sank into the earth and no one could tell where they had stood. The old woman feared that if Gerda should see the roses, she would then think of her own, would remember little Kay, and run away from her.

She now led Gerda into the flower-garden. Oh, what odour and what loveliness was there! Every flower that one could think of, and of every season, stood there in fullest bloom; no picture-book could be gayer or more beautiful. Gerda jumped for joy, and played till the sun set behind the tall cherry-tree; she then had a pretty bed, with a red silken coverlet filled with blue violets. She fell asleep, and had as pleasant dreams as ever a queen on her wedding-day.

The next morning she went to play with the flowers in the warm sunshine, and thus passed away a day. Gerda knew every flower; and, numerous as they were, it still seemed to Gerda that one was wanting, though she did not know which. One day while she was looking at the hat of the old woman painted with flowers, the most beautiful of them all seemed to her to be a rose. The old woman had forgotten to take it from her hat when she made the others vanish in the earth. But so it is when one's thoughts are not collected. "What!" said Gerda. "Are there no roses here?" and she ran about amongst the flowerbeds, and looked, and looked, but there was not one to be found. She then sat down and wept; but her hot tears fell just where a rose-bush had sunk; and when her warm tears watered the ground, the tree shot up suddenly as fresh and blooming as when it had been swallowed up. Gerda kissed the roses, thought of her own dear roses at home, and with them of little Kay.

"Oh, how long I have stayed!" said the little girl. "I intended to look for Kay! Don't you know where he is?" she asked of the roses. "Do you think he is dead and gone?"

"Dead he certainly is not," said the Roses. "We have been in the earth where all the dead are, but Kay was not there."

"Many thanks!" said little Gerda; and she went to the other flowers, looked into their cups, and asked, "Don't you know where little Kay is?"

But every flower stood in the sunshine, and dreamed its own fairy tale or its own story: and they all told her very many things, but not one knew anything of Kay.

Well, what did the Tiger-Lily say?

"Hearest thou not the drum? Bum! Bum! Those are the only two tones. Always bum! Bum! Hark to the plaintive song of the old woman, to the call of the priests! The Hindoo woman in her long robe stands upon the funeral pile; the flames rise around her and her dead husband, but the Hindoo woman thinks on the living one in the surrounding circle; on him whose eyes burn hotter than the flames—on him, the fire of whose eyes pierces her heart more than the flames which soon will burn her body to ashes. Can the heart's flame die in the flame of the funeral pile?"

"I don't understand that at all," said little Gerda.

"That is my story," said the Lily.

What did the Convolvulus say?

"Projecting over a narrow mountain-path there hangs an old feudal castle. Thick evergreens grow on the dilapidated walls, and around the altar, where a lovely maiden is standing: she bends over the railing and looks out upon the rose. No fresher rose hangs on the branches than she; no appleblossom carried away by the wind is more buoyant! How her silken robe is rustling!

"'Is he not yet come?'"

"Is it Kay that you mean?" asked little Gerda.

"I am speaking about my story—about my dream," answered the Convolvulus.

What did the Snowdrops say?

"Between the trees a long board is hanging—it is a swing. Two little girls are sitting in it, and swing themselves backwards and forwards; their frocks are as white as snow, and long green silk ribands flutter from their bonnets. Their brother, who is older than they are, stands up in the swing; he twines his arms round the cords to hold himself fast, for in one hand he has a little cup, and in the other a clay-pipe. He is blowing soap-bubbles. The swing moves, and the bubbles float in charming changing colors: the last is still hanging to the end of the pipe, and rocks in the breeze. The swing moves. The little black dog, as light as a soap-bubble, jumps up on his hind legs to try to get into the swing. It moves, the dog falls down, barks, and is angry. They tease him; the bubble bursts! A swing, a bursting bubble—such is my song!"

"What you relate may be very pretty, but you tell it in so melancholy a manner, and do not mention Kay."

What do the Hyacinths say?

"There were once upon a time three sisters, quite transparent, and very beautiful. The robe of the one was red, that of the second blue, and that of the third white. They danced hand in hand beside the calm lake in the clear moonshine. They were not elfin maidens, but mortal children. A sweet fragrance was smelt, and the maidens vanished in the wood; the fragrance grew stronger—three coffins, and in them three lovely maidens, glided out of the forest and across the lake: the shining glow-worms flew around like little floating lights. Do the dancing maidens sleep, or are they dead? The odour of the flowers says they are corpses; the evening bell tolls for the dead!"

"You make me quite sad," said little Gerda. "I cannot help thinking of the dead maidens. Oh! is little Kay really dead? The Roses have been in the earth, and they say no."

"Ding, dong!" sounded the Hyacinth bells. "We do not toll for little Kay; we do not know him. That is our way of singing, the only one we have."

And Gerda went to the Ranunculuses, that looked forth from among the shining green leaves.

"You are a little bright sun!" said Gerda. "Tell me if you know where I can find my playfellow."

And the Ranunculus shone brightly, and looked again at Gerda. What song could the Ranunculus sing? It was one that said nothing about Kay either.

"In a small court the bright sun was shining in the first days of spring. The beams glided down the white walls of a neighbor's house, and close by the fresh yellow flowers were growing, shining like gold in the warm sun-rays. An old grandmother was sitting in the air; her grand-daughter, the poor and lovely servant just come for a short visit. She knows her grandmother. There was gold, pure virgin gold in that blessed kiss. There, that is my little story," said the Ranunculus.

"My poor old grandmother!" sighed Gerda. "Yes, she is longing for me, no doubt: she is sorrowing for me, as she did for little Kay. But I will soon come home, and then I will bring Kay with me. It is of no use asking the flowers; they only know their own old rhymes, and can tell me nothing." And she tucked up her frock, to enable her to run quicker; but the Narcissus gave her a knock on the leg, just as she was going to jump over it. So she stood still, looked at the long yellow flower, and asked, "You perhaps know something?" and she bent down to the Narcissus. And what did it say?

"I can see myself—I can see myself! Oh, how odorous I am! Up in the little garret there stands, half-dressed, a little Dancer. She stands now on one leg, now on both; she despises the whole world; yet she lives only in imagi- nation. She pours water out of the teapot over a piece of stuff which she holds in her hand; it is the bodice;

cleanliness is a fine thing. The white dress is hanging on the hook; it was washed in the teapot, and dried on the roof. She puts it on, ties a saffron-colored kerchief round her neck, and then the gown looks whiter. I can see myself—I can see myself!"

"That's nothing to me," said little Gerda. "That does not concern me." And then off she ran to the further end of the garden.

The gate was locked, but she shook the rusted bolt till it was loosened, and the gate opened; and little Gerda ran off barefooted into the wide world. She looked round her thrice, but no one followed her. At last she could run no longer; she sat down on a large stone, and when she looked about her, she saw that the summer had passed; it was late in the autumn, but that one could not remark in the beautiful garden, where there was always sunshine, and where there were flowers the whole year round.

"Dear me, how long I have staid!" said Gerda. "Autumn is come. I must not rest any longer." And she got up to go further.

Oh, how tender and wearied her little feet were! All around it looked so cold and raw: the long willow-leaves were quite yellow, and the fog dripped from them like water; one leaf fell after the other: the sloes only stood full of fruit, which set one's teeth on edge. Oh, how dark and comfortless it was in the dreary world!

The Prince and Princess

Gerda was obliged to rest herself again, when, exactly opposite to her, a large Raven came hopping over the white snow. He had long been looking at Gerda and shaking his head; and now he said, "Caw! Caw!" Good day! Good day! He could not say it better; but he felt a sympathy for the little girl, and asked her where she was going all alone. The word "alone" Gerda understood quite well, and felt how much was expressed by it; so she told the Raven her whole history, and asked if he had not seen Kay.

The Raven nodded very gravely, and said, "It may be—it may be!"

"What, do you really think so?" cried the little girl; and she nearly squeezed the Raven to death, so much did she kiss him.

"Gently, gently," said the Raven. "I think I know; I think that it may be little Kay. But now he has forgotten you for the Princess."

"Does he live with a Princess?" asked Gerda.

"Yes—listen," said the Raven; "but it will be difficult for me to speak your language. If you understand the Raven language I can tell you better."

"No, I have not learnt it," said Gerda; "but my grandmother understands it, and she can speak gibberish too. I wish I had learnt it."

"No matter," said the Raven; "I will tell you as well as I can; however, it will be bad enough." And then he told all he knew.

"In the kingdom where we now are there lives a Princess, who is extraordinarily clever; for she has read all the newspapers in the whole world, and has forgotten them again—so clever is she. She was lately, it is said, sitting on her throne—which is not very amusing after all—when she began humming an old tune, and it was just, 'Oh, why should I not be married?' 'That song is not without its meaning,' said she, and so then she was determined to marry; but she would have a husband who knew how to give an answer when he was spoken to—not one who looked only as if he were a great personage, for that is so tiresome. She then had all the ladies of the court drummed together; and when they heard her intention, all were very pleased, and said, 'We are very glad to hear it; it is the very thing we were thinking of.' You may believe every word I say," said the Raven; "for I have a tame sweetheart that hops about in the palace quite free, and it was she who told me all this.

"The newspapers appeared forthwith with a border of hearts and the initials of the Princess; and therein you might read that every good-looking young man was at liberty to come to the palace and speak to the Princess; and he who spoke in such wise as showed he felt himself at home there, that one the Princess would choose for her husband.

"Yes, Yes," said the Raven, "you may believe it; it is as true as I am sitting here. People came in crowds; there was a crush and a hurry, but no one was successful either on the first or second day. They could all talk well enough when they were out in the street; but as soon as they came inside the palace gates, and saw the guard richly dressed in silver, and the lackeys in gold on the staircase, and the large illuminated saloons, then they were abashed; and when they stood before the throne on which the Princess was sitting, all they could do was to repeat the last word they had uttered, and to hear it again did not interest her very much. It was just as if the people within were under a charm, and had fallen into a trance till they came out again into the street; for then—oh, then—they could chatter enough. There was a whole row of them standing from the town-gates to the palace. I was there myself to look," said the Raven. "They grew hungry and thirsty; but from the palace they got nothing whatever, not even a glass of water. Some of the cleverest, it is true, had taken bread and butter with them: but none shared it with his neighbor, for each thought, 'Let him look hungry, and then the Princess won't have him.'"

"But Kay—little Kay," said Gerda, "when did he come? Was he among the number?"

"Patience, patience; we are just come to him. It was on the third day when a little personage without horse or equipage, came marching right boldly up to the palace; his eyes shone like yours, he had beautiful long hair, but his clothes were very shabby."

"That was Kay," cried Gerda, with a voice of delight. "Oh, now I've found him!" and she clapped her hands for joy.

"He had a little knapsack at his back," said the Raven.

"No, that was certainly his sledge," said Gerda; "for when he went away he took his sledge with him."

"That may be," said the Raven; "I did not examine him so minutely; but I know from my tame sweetheart, that when he came into the court-yard of the palace, and saw the body-guard in silver, the lackeys on the staircase, he was not the least abashed; he nodded, and said to them, 'It must be very tiresome to stand on the stairs; for my part, I shall go in.' The saloons were gleaming with lustres—privy councillors and excellencies were walking about barefooted, and wore gold keys; it was enough to make any one feel uncomfortable. His boots creaked, too, so loudly, but still he was not at all afraid."

"That's Kay for certain," said Gerda. "I know he had on new boots; I have heard them creaking in grandmama's room."

"Yes, they creaked," said the Raven. "And on he went boldly up to the Princess, who was sitting on a pearl as large as a spinning-wheel. All the ladies of the court, with their attendants and attendants' attendants, and all the cavaliers, with their gentlemen and gentlemen's gentlemen, stood round; and the nearer they stood to the door, the prouder they looked. It was hardly possible to look at the gentleman's gentleman, so very haughtily did he stand in the doorway."

"It must have been terrible," said little Gerda. "And did Kay get the Princess?"

"Were I not a Raven, I should have taken the Princess myself, although I am promised. It is said he spoke as well as I speak when I talk Raven language; this I learned from my tame sweetheart. He was bold and nicely behaved; he had not come to woo the Princess, but only to hear her wisdom. She pleased him, and he pleased her."

"Yes, yes; for certain that was Kay," said Gerda. "He was so clever; he could reckon fractions in his head. Oh, won't you take me to the palace?"

"That is very easily said," answered the Raven. "But how are we to manage it? I'll speak to my tame sweetheart about it: she must advise us; for so much I must tell you, such a little girl as you are will never get permission to enter."

"Oh, yes I shall," said Gerda; "when Kay hears that I am here, he will come out directly to fetch me."

"Wait for me here on these steps," said the Raven. He moved his head backwards and forwards and flew away.

The evening was closing in when the Raven returned. "Caw—caw!" said he. "She sends you her compliments; and here is a roll for you. She took it out of the kitchen, where there is bread enough. You are hungry, no doubt. It is not possible for you to enter the palace, for you are barefooted: the guards in silver, and the lackeys in gold, would not allow it; but do not cry, you shall come in still. My sweetheart knows a little back stair that leads to the bedchamber, and she knows where she can get the key of it."

And they went into the garden in the large avenue, where one leaf was falling after the other; and when the lights in the palace had all gradually disappeared, the

Raven led little Gerda to the back door, which stood half open.

Oh, how Gerda's heart beat with anxiety and longing! It was just as if she had been about to do something wrong; and yet she only wanted to know if little Kay was there. Yes, he must be there. She called to mind his intelligent eyes, and his long hair, so vividly, she could quite see him as he used to laugh when they were sitting under the roses at home. "He will, no doubt, be glad to see you—to hear what a long way you have come for his sake; to know how unhappy all at home were when he did not come back."

Oh, what a fright and a joy it was!

They were now on the stairs. A single lamp was burning there; and on the floor stood the tame Raven, turning her head on every side and looking at Gerda, who bowed as her grandmother had taught her to do.

"My intended has told me so much good of you, my dear young lady," said the tame Raven. "Your tale is very affecting. If you will take the lamp, I will go before. We will go straight on, for we shall meet no one."

"I think there is somebody just behind us," said Gerda; and something rushed past: it was like shadowy figures on the wall; horses with flowing manes and thin legs, huntsmen, ladies and gentlemen on horseback.

"They are only dreams," said the Raven. "They come to fetch the thoughts of the high personages to the chase; 'tis well, for now you can observe them in bed all the better. But let me find, when you enjoy honor and distinction, that you possess a grateful heart."

"Tut! That's not worth talking about," said the Raven of the woods.

They now entered the first saloon, which was of rose-colored satin, with artificial flowers on the wall. Here the dreams were rushing past, but they hastened by so quickly that Gerda could not see the high personages. One hall was more magnificent than the other; one might indeed well be abashed; and at last they came into the bedchamber. The ceiling of the room resembled a large palm-tree with leaves of glass, of costly glass; and in the middle, from a thick golden stem, hung two beds, each of which resembled a lily. One was white, and in this lay the Princess; the other was red, and it was here that Gerda was to look for little Kay. She bent back one of the red leaves, and saw a brown neck. Oh! that was Kay! She called him quite loud by name, held the lamp towards him—the dreams rushed back again into the chamber—he awoke, turned his head, and—it was not little Kay!

The Prince was only like him about the neck; but he was young and handsome. And out of the white lily leaves the Princess peeped, too, and asked what was the matter. Then little Gerda cried, and told her her whole history, and all that the Ravens had done for her.

"Poor little thing!" said the Prince and the Princess. They praised the Ravens very much, and told them they were not at all angry with them, but they were not to do so again. However, they should have a reward. "Will you fly about here at liberty," asked the Princess; "or would you like to have a fixed appointment as court ravens, with all the broken bits from the kitchen?"

And both the Ravens nodded, and begged for a fixed appointment; for they thought of their old age, and said, "It is a good thing to have a provision for our old days."

And the Prince got up and let Gerda sleep in his bed, and more than this he could not do. She folded her little hands and thought, "How good men and animals are!" and she then fell asleep and slept soundly. All the dreams flew in again, and they now looked like the angels; they drew a little sledge, in which little Kay sat and nodded his head; but the whole was only a dream, and therefore it all vanished as soon as she awoke.

The next day she was dressed from head to foot in silk and velvet. They offered to let her stay at the palace, and lead a happy life; but she begged to have a little carriage with a horse in front, and for a small pair of shoes; then, she said, she would again go forth in the wide world and look for Kay.

Shoes and a muff were given her; she was, too, dressed very nicely; and when she was about to set off, a new carriage stopped before the door. It was of pure gold, and the arms of the Prince and Princess shone like a star upon it; the coachman, the footmen, and the outriders, for outriders were there, too, all wore golden crowns. The Prince and the Princess assisted her into the carriage themselves, and wished her all success. The Raven of the woods, who was now married, accompanied her for the first three miles. He sat beside Gerda, for he could not bear riding backwards; the other Raven stood in the doorway, and flapped her wings; she could not accompany Gerda, because she suffered from headache since she had had a fixed appointment and ate so much. The carriage was lined inside with sugar-plums, and in the seats were fruits and gingerbread.

"Farewell! Farewell!" cried Prince and Princess; and Gerda wept, and the Raven wept. Thus passed the first miles; and then the Raven bade her farewell, and this was the most painful separation of all. He flew into a tree, and beat his black wings as long as he could see the carriage, that shone from afar like a sunbeam.

The Little Robber Maiden

They drove through the dark wood; but the carriage shone like a torch, and it dazzled the eyes of the robbers, so that they could not bear to look at it.

"'Tis gold! 'Tis gold!" they cried; and they rushed forward, seized the horses, knocked down the little postilion, the coachman, and the servants, and pulled little Gerda out of the carriage.

"How plump, how beautiful she is! She must have been fed on nut-kernels," said the old female robber, who had a long, scrubby beard, and bushy eyebrows that hung down over her eyes. "She is as good as a fatted lamb! How nice she will be!" And then she drew out a knife, the blade of which shone so that it was quite dreadful to behold.

"Oh!" cried the woman at the same moment. She had been bitten in the ear by her own little daughter, who hung at her back; and who was so wild and unmanageable, that it was quite amusing to see her. "You naughty child!" said the mother: and now she had not time to kill Gerda.

"She shall play with me," said the little robber child. "She shall give me her muff, and her pretty frock; she shall sleep in my bed!" And then she gave her mother another bite, so that she jumped, and ran round with the pain; and the Robbers laughed, and said, "Look, how she is dancing with the little one!"

"I will go into the carriage," said the little robber maiden; and she would have her will, for she was very spoiled and very headstrong. She and Gerda got in; and then away they drove over the stumps of felled trees, deeper and deeper into the woods. The little robber maiden was as tall as Gerda, but stronger, broader-shouldered, and of dark complexion; her eyes were quite black; they looked almost melancholy. She embraced little Gerda, and said, "They shall not kill you as long as I am not displeased with you. You are, doubtless, a Princess?"

"No," said little Gerda; who then related all that had happened to her, and how much she cared about little Kay.

The little robber maiden looked at her with a serious air, nodded her head slightly, and said, "They shall not kill you, even if I am angry with you: then I will do it myself"; and she dried Gerda's eyes, and put both her hands in the handsome muff, which was so soft and warm.

At length the carriage stopped. They were in the midst of the court-yard of a robber's castle. It was full of cracks from top to bottom; and out of the openings magpies and rooks were flying; and the great bull-dogs, each of which looked as if he could swallow a man, jumped up, but they did not bark, for that was forbidden.

In the midst of the large, old, smoking hall burnt a great fire on the stone floor. The smoke disappeared under the stones, and had to seek its own egress. In an immense caldron soup was boiling; and rabbits and hares were being roasted on a spit.

"You shall sleep with me to-night, with all my animals," said the little robber maiden. They had something to eat and drink; and then went into a corner, where straw and carpets were lying. Beside them, on laths and perches, sat nearly a hundred pigeons, all asleep, seemingly; but yet they moved a little when the robber maiden came. "They are all mine," said she, at the same time seizing one that was next to her by the legs and shaking it so that its wings fluttered. "Kiss it," cried the little girl, and flung the pigeon in Gerda's face. "Up there is the rabble of the wood," continued she, pointing to several laths which were fastened before a hole high up in the wall; "that's the rabble; they would all fly away immediately, if they were not well fastened in. And here is my dear old Bac"; and she laid hold of the horns of a reindeer, that had a bright copper ring round its neck, and was tethered to the spot.

"We are obliged to lock this fellow in too, or he would make his escape. Every evening I tickle his neck with my sharp knife; he is so frightened at it!" and the little girl drew forth a long knife, from a crack in the wall, and let it glide over the Reindeer's neck. The poor animal kicked; the girl laughed, and pulled Gerda into bed with her.

"Do you intend to keep your knife while you sleep?" asked Gerda; looking at it rather fearfully.

"I always sleep with the knife," said the little robber maiden. "There is no knowing what may happen. But tell me now, once more, all about little Kay; and why you have started off in the wide world alone." And Gerda related all, from the very beginning: the Wood-pigeons cooed above in their cage, and the others slept. The little robber maiden wound her arm round Gerda's neck, held the knife in the other hand, and snored so loud that everybody could hear her; but Gerda could not close her eyes, for she did not know whether she was to live or die. The robbers sat round the fire, sang and drank; and the old female robber jumped about so, that it was quite dreadful for Gerda to see her.

Then the Wood-pigeons said, "Coo! Coo! We have seen little Kay! A white hen carries his sledge; he himself sat in the carriage of the Snow Queen, who passed here, down just over the wood, as we lay in our nest. She blew upon us young ones; and all died except we two. Coo! Coo!"

"What is that you say up there?" cried little Gerda. "Where did the Snow Queen go to? Do you know anything about it?"

"She is no doubt gone to Lapland; for there is always snow and ice there. Only ask the Reindeer, who is tethered there."

"Ice and snow is there! There it is, glorious and beautiful!" said the Reindeer. "One can spring about in the large shining valleys! The Snow Queen has her summer-tent there; but her fixed abode is high up towards the North Pole, on the Island called Spitzbergen."

"Oh, Kay! Poor little Kay!" sighed Gerda.

"Do you choose to be quiet?" said the robber maiden. "If you don't, I shall make you."

In the morning Gerda told her all that the Wood-pigeons had said; and the little maiden looked very serious, but she nodded her head, and said, "That's no matter—that's no matter. Do you know where Lapland lies!" she asked of the Reindeer.

"Who should know better than I?" said the animal; and his eyes rolled in his head. "I was born and bred there—there I leapt about on the fields of snow."

"Listen," said the robber maiden to Gerda. "You see that the men are gone; but my mother is still here, and will remain. However, towards morning she takes a draught out of the large flask, and then she sleeps a little: then I will do something for you." She now jumped out of bed, flew to her mother; with her arms round her neck, and pulling her by the beard, said, "Good morrow, my own sweet nanny-goat of a mother." And her mother took hold of her nose, and pinched it till it was red and blue; but this was all done out of pure love.

When the mother had taken a sup at her flask, and was having a nap, the little robber maiden went to the Reindeer, and said, "I should very much like to give you still many a tickling with the sharp knife, for then you are so amusing; however, I will untether you, and help you out, so that you may go back to Lapland. But you must make good use of your legs; and take this little girl for me to the palace of the Snow Queen, where her playfellow is. You have heard, I suppose, all she said; for she spoke loud enough, and you were listening."

The Reindeer gave a bound for joy. The robber maiden lifted up little Gerda, and took the precaution to bind her fast on the Reindeer's back; she even gave her a small cushion to sit on. "Here are your worsted leggins, for it will be cold; but the muff I shall keep for myself, for it is so very pretty. But I do not wish you to be cold. Here is a pair of lined gloves of my mother's; they just reach up to your elbow. On with them! Now you look about the hands just like my ugly old mother!"

And Gerda wept for joy.

"I can't bear to see you fretting," said the little robber maiden. "This is just the time when you ought to look pleased. Here are two loaves and a ham for you, so that you won't starve." The bread and the meat were fastened to the Reindeer's back; the little maiden opened the door, called in all the dogs, and then with her knife cut the rope that fastened the animal, and said to him, "Now, off with you; but take good care of the little girl!"

And Gerda stretched out her hands with the large wadded gloves towards the robber maiden, and said, "Farewell!" and the Reindeer flew on over bush and bramble through the great wood, over moor and heath, as fast as he could go.

"Ddsa! Ddsa!" was heard in the sky. It was just as if somebody was sneezing.

"These are my old northern-lights," said the Reindeer, "look how they gleam!" And on he now sped still quicker— day and night on he went: the loaves were consumed, and the ham too; and now they were in Lapland.

The Lapland Woman and the Finland Woman

Suddenly they stopped before a little house, which looked very miserable. The roof reached to the ground; and the door was so low, that the family were obliged to creep upon their stomachs when they went in or out. Nobody was at home except an old Lapland woman, who was dressing fish by the light of an oil lamp. And the Reindeer told her the whole of Gerda's history, but first of all his own; for that seemed to him of much greater importance. Gerda was so chilled that she could not speak.

"Poor thing," said the Lapland woman, "you have far to run still. You have more than a hundred miles to go before you get to Finland; there the Snow Queen has her country-house, and burns blue lights every evening. I will give you a few words from me, which I will write on a dried haberdine, for paper I have none; this you can take with you to the Finland woman, and she will be able to give you more information than I can."

When Gerda had warmed herself, and had eaten and drunk, the Lapland woman wrote a few words on a dried haberdine, begged Gerda to take care of them, put her on the Reindeer, bound her fast, and away sprang the animal. "Ddsa! Ddsa!" was again heard in the air; the most charming blue lights burned the whole night in the sky, and at last they came to Finland. They knocked at the chimney of the Finland woman; for as to a door, she had none.

There was such a heat inside that the Finland woman herself went about almost naked. She was diminutive and dirty. She immediately loosened little Gerda's clothes, pulled off her thick gloves and boots; for otherwise the heat would have been too great—and after laying a piece of ice on the Reindeer's head, read what was written on the fish-skin. She read it three times: she then knew it by heart; so she put the fish into the cupboard—for it might very well be eaten, and she never threw anything away.

Then the Reindeer related his own story first, and afterwards that of little Gerda; and the Finland woman winked her eyes, but said nothing.

"You are so clever," said the Reindeer; "you can, I know, twist all the winds of the world together in a knot. If the seaman loosens one knot, then he has a good wind; if a second, then it blows pretty stiffly; if he undoes the third and fourth, then it rages so that the forests are upturned. Will you give the little maiden a potion, that she may possess the strength of twelve men, and vanquish the Snow Queen?"

"The strength of twelve men!" said the Finland woman. "Much good that would be!" Then she went to a cupboard, and drew out a large skin rolled up. When she had unrolled it, strange characters were to be seen written thereon; and the Finland woman read at such a rate that the perspiration trickled down her forehead.

But the Reindeer begged so hard for little Gerda, and Gerda looked so imploringly with tearful eyes at the Finland woman, that she winked, and drew the Reindeer aside into a corner, where they whispered together, while the animal got some fresh ice put on his head.

"'Tis true little Kay is at the Snow Queen's, and finds everything there quite to his taste; and he thinks it the very best place in the world; but the reason of that is, he has a splinter of glass in his eye, and in his heart. These must be got out first; otherwise he will never go back to mankind, and the Snow Queen will retain her power over him."

"But can you give little Gerda nothing to take which will endue her with power over the whole?"

"I can give her no more power than what she has already. Don't you see how great it is? Don't you see how men and animals are forced to serve her; how well she gets through the world barefooted? She must not hear of her power from us; that power lies in her heart, because she is a sweet and innocent child! If she cannot get to the Snow Queen by herself, and rid little Kay of the glass, we cannot help her. Two miles hence the garden of the Snow Queen begins; thither you may carry the little girl. Set her down by the large bush with red berries, standing in the snow; don't stay talking, but hasten back as fast as possible." And now the Finland woman placed little Gerda on the Reindeer's back, and off he ran with all imaginable speed.

"Oh! I have not got my boots! I have not brought my gloves!" cried little Gerda. She remarked she was without them from the cutting frost; but the Reindeer dared not stand still; on he ran till he came to the great bush with the red berries, and there he set Gerda down, kissed her mouth, while large bright tears flowed from the animal's eyes, and then back he went as fast as possible. There stood poor Gerda now, without shoes or gloves, in the very middle of dreadful icy Finland.

She ran on as fast as she could. There then came a whole regiment of snow-flakes, but they did not fall from above, and they were quite bright and shining from the Aurora Borealis. The flakes ran along the ground, and the nearer they came the larger they grew. Gerda well remembered how large and strange the snow-flakes appeared when she once saw them through a magnifying-glass; but now they were large and terrific in another manner—they were all alive. They were the outposts of the Snow Queen. They had the most wondrous shapes; some looked like large ugly porcupines; others like snakes knotted together, with their heads sticking out; and others, again, like small fat bears, with the hair standing on end: all were of dazzling whiteness—all were living snow-flakes.

Little Gerda repeated the Lord's Prayer. The cold was so intense that she could see her own breath, which came like smoke out of her mouth. It grew thicker and thicker, and took the form of little angels, that grew more and more when they touched the earth. All had helms on their heads, and lances and shields in their hands; they increased in numbers; and when Gerda had finished the Lord's Prayer, she was surrounded by a whole legion. They thrust at the horrid snow-flakes with their spears, so that they flew into a thousand pieces; and little Gerda walked on bravely and in security. The angels patted her hands and feet; and then she felt the cold less, and went on quickly towards the palace of the Snow Queen.

But now we shall see how Kay fared. He never thought of Gerda, and least of all that she was standing before the palace.

What Took Place in the Palace of the Snow Queen, and What Happened Afterward

The walls of the palace were of driving snow, and the windows and doors of cutting winds. There were more than a hundred halls there, according as the snow was driven by the winds. The largest was many miles in extent; all were lighted up by the powerful Aurora Borealis, and all were so large, so empty, so icy cold, and so resplendent! Mirth never reigned there; there was never even a little bear-ball, with the storm for music, while the polar bears went on their hind legs and showed off their steps. Never a little tea-party of white young lady foxes; vast, cold, and empty were the halls of the Snow Queen. The northern-lights shone with such precision that one could tell exactly when they were at their highest or lowest degree of brightness. In the middle of the empty, endless hall of snow, was a frozen lake; it was cracked in a thousand pieces, but each piece was so like the other, that it seemed the work of a cunning artificer. In the middle of this lake sat the Snow Queen when she was at home; and then she said she was sitting in the Mirror of Understanding, and that this was the only one and the best thing in the world.

Little Kay was quite blue, yes nearly black with cold; but he did not observe it, for she had kissed away all feeling of cold from his body, and his heart was a lump of ice. He was dragging along some pointed flat pieces of ice, which he laid together in all possible ways, for he wanted to make something with them; just as we have little flat pieces of wood to make geometrical figures with, called the Chinese Puzzle. Kay made all sorts of figures, the most complicated, for it was an ice-puzzle for the understanding. In his eyes the figures were extraordinarily beautiful, and of the utmost importance; for the bit of glass which was in his eye caused this. He found whole figures which represented a written word; but he never could manage to represent just the word he wanted—that word was "eternity"; and the Snow Queen had said, "If you can discover that figure, you shall be your own master, and I will make you a present of the whole world and a pair of new skates." But he could not find it out.

"I am going now to warm lands," said the Snow Queen. "I must have a look down into the black caldrons." It was the volcanoes Vesuvius and Etna that she meant. "I will just give them a coating of white, for that is as it ought to be; besides, it is good for the oranges and the grapes." And then away she flew, and Kay sat quite alone in the empty halls of ice that were miles long, and looked at the blocks of ice, and thought and thought till his skull was almost cracked. There he sat quite benumbed and motionless; one would have imagined he was frozen to death.

Suddenly little Gerda stepped through the great portal into the palace. The gate was formed of cutting winds; but Gerda repeated her evening prayer, and the winds were laid as though they slept; and the little maiden entered the vast, empty, cold halls. There she beheld Kay: she recognised him, flew to embrace him, and cried out, her arms firmly holding him the while, "Kay, sweet little Kay! Have I then found you at last?"

But he sat quite still, benumbed and cold. Then little Gerda shed burning tears; and they fell on his bosom, they penetrated to his heart, they thawed the lumps of ice, and consumed the splinters of the looking-glass; he looked at her, and she sang the hymn:

"The rose in the valley is blooming so sweet, And angels descend there the children to greet."

Hereupon Kay burst into tears; he wept so much that the splinter rolled out of his eye, and he recognised her, and shouted, "Gerda, sweet little Gerda! Where have you been so long? And where have I been?" He looked round him. "How cold it is here!" said he. "How empty and cold!" And he held fast by Gerda, who laughed and wept for joy. It was so beautiful, that even the blocks of ice danced about for joy; and when they were tired and laid themselves down, they formed exactly the letters which the Snow Queen had told him to find out; so now he was his own master, and he would have the whole world and a pair of new skates into the bargain.

Gerda kissed his cheeks, and they grew quite blooming; she kissed his eyes, and they shone like her own; she kissed his hands and feet, and he was again well and merry. The Snow Queen might come back as soon as she liked; there stood his discharge written in resplendent masses of ice.

They took each other by the hand, and wandered forth out of the large hall; they talked of their old grandmother, and of the roses upon the roof; and wherever they went, the winds ceased raging, and the sun burst forth. And when they reached the bush with the red berries, they found the Reindeer waiting for them. He had brought another, a young one, with him, whose udder was filled with milk, which he gave to the little ones, and kissed their lips. They then carried Kay and Gerda—first to the Finland woman, where they warmed themselves in the warm room, and learned what they were to do on their journey home; and they went to the Lapland woman, who made some new clothes for them and repaired their sledges.

The Reindeer and the young hind leaped along beside them, and accompanied them to the boundary of the country. Here the first vegetation peeped forth; here Kay and Gerda took leave of the Lapland woman. "Farewell! Farewell!" they all said. And the first green buds appeared, the first little birds began to chirrup; and out of the wood came, riding on a magnificent horse, which Gerda knew (it was one of the leaders in the golden carriage), a young damsel with a bright-red cap on her head, and armed with pistols. It was the little robber maiden, who, tired of being at home, had determined to make a journey to the north; and afterwards in another direction, if that did not please her. She recognised Gerda immediately, and Gerda knew her too. It was a joyful meeting.

"You are a fine fellow for tramping about," said she to little Kay; "I should like to know, faith, if you deserve that one should run from one end of the world to the other for your sake?"

But Gerda patted her cheeks, and inquired for the Prince and Princess.

"They are gone abroad," said the other.

"But the Raven?" asked little Gerda.

"Oh! The Raven is dead," she answered. "His tame sweetheart is a widow, and wears a bit of black worsted round her leg; she laments most piteously, but it's all mere talk and stuff! Now tell me what you've been doing and how you managed to catch him."

And Gerda and Kay both told their story.

And "Schnipp-schnapp-schnurre-basselurre," said the

robber maiden; and she took the hands of each, and promised that if she should some day pass through the town where they lived, she would come and visit them; and then away she rode. Kay and Gerda took each other's hand: it was lovely spring weather, with abundance of flowers and of verdure. The church-bells rang, and the children recognised the high towers, and the large town; it was that in which they dwelt. They entered and hastened up to their grandmother's room, where everything was standing as formerly. The clock said "tick! tack!" and the finger moved round; but as they entered, they remarked that they were now grown up. The roses on the leads hung blooming in at the open window; there stood the little children's chairs, and Kay and Gerda sat down on them, holding each other by the hand; they both had forgotten the cold empty splendor of the Snow Queen, as though it had been a dream. The grandmother sat in the bright sunshine, and read aloud from the Bible: "Unless ye become as little children, ye cannot enter the kingdom of heaven."

And Kay and Gerda looked in each other's eyes, and all at once they understood the old hymn:

"The rose in the valley is blooming so sweet, And angels descend there the children to greet."

There sat the two grown-up persons; grown-up, and yet children; children at least in heart; and it was summer-time; summer, glorious summer!

The Fairy Goldsmith

By Elinor Wylie

Here's a wonderful thing,
A humming-bird's wing
   In hammered gold,
And store well chosen
Of snowflakes frozen
   In crystal cold.

Black onyx cherries
And mistletoe berries
   Of chrysoprase,
Jade buds, tight shut,
All carven and cut
   In intricate ways.

Here, if you please
Are little gilt bees
   In amber drops
Which look like honey,
Translucent and sunny,
   From clover-tops.

Here's an elfin girl
Of mother-of-pearl
   And moonshine made,
With tortoise-shell hair
Both dusky and fair
In its light and shade.

Here's lacquer laid thin,
Like a scarlet skin
   On an ivory fruit;
And a filigree frost
Of frail notes lost
   From a fairy lute.

Here's a turquoise chain
Of sun-shower rain
   To wear if you wish;
And glimmering green
With aquamarine,
   A silvery fish.

Here are pearls all strung
On a thread among
   Pretty pink shells;
And bubbles blown
From the opal stone
   Which ring like bells.

Touch them and take them,
But do not break them!
    Beneath your hand
They will wither like foam
If you carry them home
    Out of fairy-land.

O, they never can last
Though you hide them fast
    From moth and from rust;
In your monstrous day
They will crumble away
    Into quicksilver dust.

The Ice Maiden

By Hans Christian Andersen

Little Rudy

Let us visit Switzerland and look around us in the glorious country of mountains, where the forest rises out of steep rocky walls; let us ascend to the dazzling snow-fields, and thence descend to the green plains, where the rivulets and brooks hasten away, foaming up, as if they feared not to vanish, as they reached the sea.

The sun beams upon the deep valley, it burns also upon the heavy masses of snow; so that after the lapse of years, they melt into shining ice-blocks, and become rolling avalanches and heaped-up glaciers.

Two of these lie in the broad clefts of the rock, under the Schreckhorn and Wetterhorn, near the little town of Grindelwald. They are so remarkable that many strangers come to gaze at them, in the summer time, from all parts of the world; they come over the high snow-covered mountains, they come from the deepest valleys, and they are obliged to ascend during many hours, and as they ascend, the valley sinks deeper and deeper, as though seen from an air-balloon.

Far around the peaks of the mountains, the clouds often hang like heavy curtains of smoke; whilst down in the valley, where the many brown wooden houses lie scattered about, a sun-beam shines, and here and there brings out a tiny spot, in radiant green, as though it were transparent. The water roars, froths and foams below, the water hums and tinkles above, and it looks as if silver ribbons were fluttering over the cliffs.

On each side of the way, as one ascends, are wooden houses; each house has a little potato-garden, and that is a necessity, for in the door-way are many little mouths. There are plenty of children, and they can consume abundance of food; they rush out of the houses, and throng about the travellers, come they on foot or in carriage. The whole horde of children traffic; the little ones offer prettily carved wooden houses, for sale, similar to those they build on the mountains. Rain or shine, the children assemble with their wares.

Some twenty years ago, there stood here, several times, a little boy, who wished to sell his toys, but he always kept aloof from the other children; he stood with serious countenance and with both hands tightly clasped around his wooden box, as if he feared it would slip away from him; but on account of this gravity, and because the boy was so small, it caused him to be remarked, and often he made the best bargain, without knowing why. His grandfather lived still higher in the mountains, and it was he who carved the pretty wooden houses. There stood in the room, an old cup-board, full of carvings; there were nut-crackers, knives, spoons, and boxes with delicate foliage, and leaping chamois; there was everything, which could rejoice a merry child's eye, but this little fellow, (he was named Rudy) looked at and desired only the old gun under the rafters. His grandfather had said, that he should have it some day, but that he must first grow big and strong enough to use it.

Small as the boy was, he was obliged to take care of the goats, and if he who can climb with them is a good guardian, well then indeed was Rudy. Why he climbed even higher than they! He loved to take the bird's nests from the trees, high in the air, for he was bold and daring; and he only smiled when he stood by the roaring water-fall, or when he heard a rolling avalanche.

He never played with the other children; he only met them, when his grandfather sent him out to sell his carvings, and Rudy took but little interest in this; he much preferred to wander about the rocks, or to sit and listen to his grandfather relate about old times and about the in-habitants of Meiringen, where he came from. He said that these people had not been there since the beginning of the world; they had come from the far North, where the race called Swedes, dwelt. To know this, was indeed great wisdom, and Rudy knew this; but he became still wiser, through the intercourse which he had with the other oc-cupants of the house—belonging to the animal race. There was a large dog, Ajola, an heir-loom from Rudy's father; and a cat, and she was of great importance to Rudy, for she had taught him to climb. "Come out on the roof!" said the cat, quite plain and distinctly, for when one is a child, and can not yet speak, one understands the hens and ducks, the cats and dogs remarkably well; they speak for us as intelligibly as father or mother. One needs but to be little, and then even grandfather's stick can neigh, and become a horse, with head, legs and tail. With some children, this knowledge slips away later than with others, and people say of these, that they are very backward, that they remain children fearfully long.— People say so many things!

"Come with me, little Rudy, out on the roof!" was about the first thing that the cat said, that Rudy understood. "It is all imagination about falling; one does not fall, when one does not fear to do so. Come, place your one paw so, and your other so! Take care of your fore-paws! Look sharp with your eyes, and give suppleness to your limbs! If there be a hole, jump, hold fast, that's the way I do!"

And Rudy did so, and that was the reason that he sat out on the roof with the cat so often; he sat with her in the tree-tops, yes, he sat on the edge of the rocks, where the cats could not come. "Higher, higher!" said the trees and bushes. "See, how we climb! how high we go, how firm we hold on, even on the outermost peaks of the rocks!"

And Rudy went generally on the mountain before the sun rose, and then he got his morning drink, the fresh, strengthening mountain air, the drink, that our Lord only can prepare, and men can read its recipe, and thus it stands written: "the fresh scent of the herbs of the mountains and the mint and thyme of the valleys."

All heaviness is imbibed by the hanging clouds, and the wind sends it out like grape-shot into the fir-woods;

the fragrant breeze becomes perfume, light and fresh and ever fresher—that was Rudy's morning drink.

The blessing bringing daughters of the Sun, the sunbeams, kissed his cheeks, and Vertigo stood and watched, but dared not approach him; and the swallows below from grandfather's house, where there were no less than seven nests, flew up to him and the goats, and they sang: "We and you! and you and we!" They brought greetings from home, even from the two hens, the only birds in the room; with whom however Rudy never had intercourse.

Little as he was, he had traveled, and not a little, for so small a boy; he was born in the Canton Valais, and had been carried from there over the mountains. Lately he had visited the Staubbach, which waves in the air like a silver gauze, before the snow decked, dazzling white mountain: "the Jungfrau." And he had been in Grindelwald, near the great glaciers; but that was a sad story. There, his mother had found her death, and, "little Rudy," so said his grandfather, "had lost his childish merriment." "When the boy was not a year old, he laughed more than he cried," so wrote his mother, "but since he was in the ice-gap, quite another mind has come over him." His grand-father did not like to speak on the subject, but every one on the mountain knew all about it.

Rudy's father had been a postilion, and the large dog in the room, had always followed him on his journeys to the lake of Geneva, over the Simplon. In the valley of the Rhone, in Canton Valais, still lived Rudy's family, on his father's side, and his father's brother was a famous chamois hunter and a well-known guide. Rudy was only a year old, when he lost his father, and his mother longed to return to her relations in Berner Oberlande. Her father lived a few hours walk from Grindelwald; he was a carver in wood, and earned enough by it to live. In the month of June, carrying her little child, she started homewards, accompanied by two chamois hunters; intending to cross the Gemmi on their way to Grindelwald. They already had accomplished the longer part of their journey, had passed the high ridges, had come to the snow-plains, they already saw the valley of their home, with its well-known wooden houses, and had now but to reach the summit of one of the great glaciers. The snow had freshly fallen and concealed a cleft,—which did not lead to the deepest abyss, where the water roared—but still deeper than man could reach. The young woman, who was holding her child, slipped, sank and was gone; one heard no cry, no sigh, nought but a little child weeping. More than an hour elapsed, before her companions could bring poles and ropes, from the nearest house, in order to afford assistance. After great exertion they drew from the ice-gap, what appeared to be two lifeless bodies; every means were employed and they succeeded in calling the child back to life, but not the mother. So the old grandfather received instead of a daughter, a daughter's son in his house; the little one, who laughed more than he wept, but, who now, seemed to have lost this custom. A change in him, had certainly taken place, in the cleft of the glacier, in the wonderful cold world; where, according to the belief of the Swiss peasant, the souls of the damned are incarcerated until the day of judgment.

Not unlike water, which after long journeying, has been compressed into blocks of green glass, the glaciers lie here, so that one huge mass of ice is heaped on the other. The rushing stream roars below and melts snow and ice; within, hollow caverns and mighty clefts open, this is a wonderful palace of ice, and in it dwells the Ice-Maiden, the Queen of the glaciers. She, the murderess, the destroyer, is half a child of air and half the powerful ruler of the streams; therefore, she had received the power, to elevate herself with the speed of the chamois to the highest pinnacle of the snow-topped mountain; where the most daring mountaineer had to hew his way, in order to take firm foot-hold. She sails up the rushing river on a slender fir-branch—springs from one cliff to another, with her long snow-white hair, fluttering around her, and with her bluish-green mantle, which resembles the water of the deep Swiss lakes.

"Crush, hold fast! the power is mine!" cried she. "They have stolen a lovely boy from me, a boy, whom I had kissed, but not kissed to death. He is again with men, he tends the goats on the mountains; he climbs up, up high, beyond the reach of all others, but not beyond mine! He is mine, I shall have him!"—

And she ordered Vertigo to fulfil her duty; it was too warm for the Ice-Maiden, in summer-time, in the green spots where the mint thrives. Vertigo arose; one came, three came, (for Vertigo had many sisters, very many of them) and the Maiden chose the strongest among those that rule within doors and without. They sit on the balusters and on the spires of the steep towers, they tread through the air as the swimmer glides through the water and entice their prey down the abyss. Vertigo and the Ice-Maiden seize on men as the polypus clutches at all within its reach. Vertigo was to gain possession of Rudy. "Yes, just catch him for me" said Vertigo. "I cannot do it! The cat, the dirty thing, has taught him her arts! The child of the race of man, possesses a power, that repulses me; I cannot get at the little boy, when he hangs by the branches over the abyss. I may tickle him on the soles of his feet or give him a box on the ear whilst he is swinging in the air, it is of no avail. I can do nothing!"

"We can do it!" said the Ice-Maiden. "You or I! I! I!"—

"No, no!" sounded back the echo of the church-bells through the mountain, like a sweet melody; it was like speech, an harmonious chorus of all the spirits of nature, mild, good, full of love, for it came from the daughters of the sun-beams, who encamped themselves every evening in a circle around the pinnacles of the mountains, and spread out their rose-coloured wings, that grow more and more red as the sun sinks, and glow over the high Alps; men call it, "the Alpine glow." When the sun is down, they enter the peaks of the rocks and sleep on the white snow, until the sun rises, and then they sally forth. Above all, they love flowers, butterflies, and men, and amongst them they had chosen little Rudy as their favourite.

"You will not catch him! You shall not have him!" said they. "I have caught and kept stronger and larger ones!" said the Ice-Maiden.

Then the daughters of the Sun sang a lay of the wanderer, whose cloak the whirlwind had torn off and carried away. The wind took the covering, but not the man. "Ye children of strength can seize, but not hold him; he is stronger, he is more spirit-like, than we; he ascends higher than the Sun, our mother! He possesses the magic word, that restrains wind and water, so that they are obliged to obey and serve him!"

So sounded cheerfully the bell-like chorus.

And every morning the sun-beams shone through the tiny window in the grandfather's house, on the quiet child. The daughters of the sun-beams kissed him, they wished to thaw him, to warm him and to carry away with them the icy kiss, which the queenly maiden of the glaciers had given him, as he lay on his dead mother's lap, in the deep icy gap, whence he was saved through a miracle.

The Journey to the New Home

Rudy was now eight years old. His father's brother, in Rhonethal, the other side of the mountain, wished to have the boy, for he thought that with him he would fare and prosper better; his grandfather perceived this and gave his consent.

Rudy must go. There were others to take leave of him, besides his grandfather; first there was Ajola, the old dog.

"Your father was post-boy and I was post-dog," said Ajola. "We have travelled up and down; I know dogs and men on the other side of the mountain. It is not my custom to speak much, but now, that we shall not have much time to converse with each other, I must talk a little more than usual. I will relate a story to you; I shall tell you how I have earned my bread, and how I have eaten it. I do not understand it and I suppose that you will not either, but it matters not, for I have discovered that the good things of this earth are not equally divided between dogs or men. All are not fitted to lie on the lap and sip milk, I have not been accustomed to it; but I saw a little dog seated in the coach with us and it occupied a person's place. The woman who was its mistress, or who belonged to its mistress, had a bottle filled with milk, out of which she fed it; it got sweet sugar biscuits too, but it would not even eat them; only snuffed at them, and so the woman ate them herself. I ran in the mud, by the side of the coach, as hungry as a dog could be; I chewed my crude thoughts, that was not right—but this is often done! If I could but have been carried on some one's knee and have been seated in a coach! But one cannot have all one desires. I have not been able to do so, neither with barking nor with yawning."

That was Ajola's speech, and Rudy seized him by the neck and kissed him on his moist mouth, and then he took the cat in his arms, but she was angry at it.

"You are getting too strong for me, and I will not use my claws against you! Just climb over the mountains, I taught you to climb! Never think that you will fall, then you are secure!"

Then the cat ran away, without letting Rudy see how her grief shone out of her eye.

The hens ran about the floor; one had lost her tail; a traveller, who wished to be a hunter, had shot it off, because the creature had taken the hen for a bird of prey!

"Rudy is going over the mountain!" said one hen. "He is always in a hurry," said the other, "and I do not care for leave-takings!" and so they both tripped away.

And the goats, too, said farewell and cried: "Mit, mit, mah!" and that was so sad.

There were two nimble guides in the neighbourhood, and they were about to cross the mountains; they were to descend to the other side of the Gemmi, and Rudy followed them on foot. This was a severe march for such a little chap, but he had strength and courage, and felt not fatigue.

The swallows accompanied them a part of the way. They sang: "We and you! You and us!" The road went over the rapid Lütschine, which rushes forth from the black clefts of the glacier of Grindelwald, in many little streams. The fallen timber and the quarry-stones serve as bridges; they pass the alder-bush and descend the mountain where the glacier has detached itself from the mountain side; they cross over the glacier, over the blocks of ice, and go around them. Rudy was obliged to creep a little, to walk a little, his eyes sparkled with delight, and he trod as firmly with his iron-shod mountain shoes, as though he wished to leave his foot-prints where he had stepped. The black mud which the mountain stream had poured upon the glacier gave it a calcined appearance, but the bluish-green, glassy ice still shone through it. They were obliged to go around the little ponds which were dammed up by blocks of ice; during these wanderings they came too near a large stone, which lay tottering on the brink of a crevice in the ice. The stone lost its equilibrium, it fell, rolled and the echo resounded from the deep hollow paths of the glacier.

Up, ever up; the glacier stretched itself on high—as a river, of wildly heaped up masses of ice, compressed among the steep cliffs. For an instant Rudy thought on what they had told him, about his having laid with his mother, in one of these cold-breathing chasms. Such thoughts soon vanished; it seemed to him as though it were some other story—one of the many which had been related to him. Now and then, when the men thought that the ascent was too difficult for the little lad, they would reach him their hand, but he was never weary and stood on the slippery ice as firm as a chamois. Now they reached the bottom of the rocks, they were soon among the bare stones, which were void of moss; soon under the low fir-trees and again out on the green common—ever changing, ever new. Around them arose the snow mountains, whose names were as familiar to Rudy as they were to every child in the neighbourhood: "the Jungfrau," "the Mönch," and "the Eiger."

Rudy had never been so high before, had never before trodden on the vast sea of snow, which lay there with its immoveable waves. The wind blew single flakes about, as it blows the foam upon the waters of the sea.

Glacier stood by glacier, if one may say so, hand in hand; each one was an ice-palace for the Ice-Maiden, whose power and will is: "to catch and to bury." The sun burned warmly, the snow was dazzling, as if sown with bluish-white, glittering diamond sparks. Countless insects (butterflies and bees mostly) lay in masses dead on the snow; they had ventured too high, or the wind had borne them thither, but to breathe their last in these cold regions. A threatening cloud hung over the Wetterhorn, like a fine, black tuft of wool. It lowered itself slowly, heavily, with that which lay concealed within it, and this was the "Föhn," powerful in its strength when it broke loose. The impression of the entire journey, the night quarters above and then the road beyond, the deep rocky chasms, where the water forced its way through the blocks of stone with terrible rapidity, engraved itself indelibly on Rudy's mind.

On the other side of the sea of snow, a forsaken stone hut gave them protection and shelter for the night; a fire was quickly lighted, for they found within it charcoal and fir branches; they arranged their couch as well as possible. The men seated themselves around the fire, smoked their tobacco and drank the warm spicy drink, which they had prepared for themselves. Rudy had his share too and they told him of the mysterious beings of the Alpine country; of the singular fighting snakes in the deep lakes; of the people of night; of the hordes of spectres, who carry sleepers through the air, towards the wonderful floating city of Venice; of the wild shepherd, who drives his black sheep over the meadow; it is true, they had never been seen, but the sound of the bells and the unhappy bellowing of the flock, had been heard.

Rudy listened eagerly, but without any fear, for he did not even know what that was, and whilst he listened he thought he heard the ghost-like hollow bellowing! Yes, it became more and more distinct, the men heard it also, they stopped talking, listened and told Rudy he must not sleep.

It was the Föhn which blew, the powerful storm-wind, which rushes down the mountains into the valley and with its strength bends the trees, as if they were mere reeds, and lifts the wooden houses from one side of the river to the other, as if the move had been made on a chess-board.

After the lapse of an hour, they told Rudy that the storm had now blown over and that he might rest; with this license, fatigued by his march, he at once fell asleep.

They departed early in the morning; the sun showed Rudy new mountains, new glaciers and snow-fields; they had now reached Canton Valais and the other side of the mountain ridge which was visible at Grindelwald, but they were still far from the new home. Other chasms, precipices, pasture-grounds; forests and paths through the woods, unfolded themselves to the view; other houses, other human beings—but what human beings! Deformed creatures, with unmeaning, fat, yellowish-white faces; with a large, ugly, fleshy lump on their necks; these were cretins who dragged themselves miserably along and gazed with their stupid eyes on the strangers who arrived among them. As for the women, the greatest number of them were frightful!

Were these the inhabitants of the new home?

The Father's Brother

The people in the uncle's house, looked, thank heaven, like those whom Rudy was accustomed to see. But one cretin was there, a poor silly lad, one of the many miserable creatures, who on account of their poverty and need, always make their home among the families of Canton Valais and remain with each but a couple of months. The wretched Saperli happened to be there when Rudy arrived.

Rudy's father's brother was still a vigorous hunter and was also a cooper by trade; his wife, a lively little person, had what is called a bird's face; her eyes resembled those of an eagle and she had a long neck entirely covered with down.

Everything was new to Rudy, the dress, manners and customs, yes, even the language, but that is soon acquired and understood by a child's ear. Here, they seemed to be better off, than in his grandfather's house; the dwelling rooms were larger, the walls looked gay with their chamois horns and highly polished rifles; over the door-way hung the picture of the blessed Virgin; alpine roses and a burning lamp stood before it.

His uncle, was as we have said before, one of the most famous chamois hunters in the neighbourhood and also the most experienced and best guide.

Rudy was to be the pet of the household, although there already was one, an old deaf and blind dog, whom they could no longer use; but they remembered his many past services and he was looked upon as a member of the family and was to pass his old days in peace. Rudy patted the dog, but he would have nothing to do with strangers; Rudy did not long remain one, for he soon took firm hold both in house and heart.

"One is not badly off in Canton Valais," said his uncle, "we have the chamois, they do not die out so soon as the mountain goat! It is a great deal better here now, than in the old times; they may talk about their glory as much as they please. The present time is much better, for a hole has been made in the purse and light and air let into our quiet valley. When old worn-out customs die away, something new springs forth!" said he. When uncle became talkative, he told of the years of his childhood and of his father's active time, when Valais was still a closed purse, as the people called it, and when it was filled with sick people and miserable cretins. French soldiers came, they were the right kind of doctors, they not only shot down the sickness but the men also.

"The Frenchmen can beat the stones until they surrender! they cut the Simplon-road out of the rocks— they have hewn out such a road, that I now can tell a three year old child to go to Italy! Keep to the highway, and a child may find his way there!" Then the uncle would sing a French song and cry hurrah for Napoleon Bonaparte.

Rudy now heard for the first time of France, of Lyons—the large city of the Rhone—for his uncle had been there.

"I wonder if Rudy will become an agile chamois hunter in a few years? He has every disposition for it!" said his uncle, and instructed him how to hold a rifle, how to aim and to fire. In the hunting season, he took him with him in the mountains and made him drink the warm chamois blood, which prevents the hunter from becoming dizzy. He taught him to heed the time when the avalanches roll down the different sides of the mountain—at mid-day or at night-fall—which depended upon the heat of the rays of the sun. He taught him to notice the chamois, in order to learn from them how to jump, so as to alight steadily upon the feet. If there was no resting place in the clefts of the rock for the foot, he must know how to support himself with the elbow, and be able to climb by means of the muscles of the thigh and calf, even the neck must serve when it is necessary. The chamois are cunning, they place out-guards—but the hunter must be still more cunning and follow the trail—and he can deceive them by hanging his coat and hat on his alpine stick, and so make the chamois take the coat for the man.

One day when Rudy was out with his uncle hunting, he tried this sport.

The rocky path was not wide; indeed there was scarcely any, only a narrow ledge, close to the dizzy abyss. The snow was half-thawed, the stones crumbled when trodden upon, and his uncle stretched himself out full length and crept along. Each stone as it broke away, fell, knocked itself, bounded and then rolled down; it made many leaps from one rocky wall to another until it found repose in the black deep. Rudy stood about a hundred steps behind his uncle on the outermost cliff, and saw a huge golden vulture, hovering over his uncle, and sailing towards him through the air, as though wishing to cast the creeping worm into the abyss with one blow of his wing, and to make carrion of him. His uncle had only eyes for the chamois and its young kid, on the other side of the cleft. Rudy looked at the bird, understood what it wanted, and laid his hand on his rifle in order to shoot it. At that moment the chamois leaped—his uncle fired—the ball hit the animal, but the kid was gone, as though flight and danger had been its life's experience. The monstrous bird terrified by the report of the gun, took flight in another direction, and Rudy's uncle knew nought of his danger, until Rudy told him of it.

As they now were on their way home in the gayest spirits—his uncle playing one of his youthful melodies on his flute—they suddenly heard not far from them a singular sound; they looked sideways, they gazed aloof and saw high above them the snow covering of the rugged shelf of the rock, waving like an outspread piece of linen when agitated by the wind. The icy waves cracked like slabs of marble, they broke, dissolved in foaming, rushing water and sounded like a muffled thunder-clap. It was an avalanche rolling down, not over Rudy and his uncle, but near, only too near to them.

"Hold fast, Rudy," cried he, "firm, with your whole strength!"

And Rudy clasped the trunk of a tree; his uncle climbed into its branches and held fast, whilst the avalanche rolled many fathoms away from them. But the air-drift of the blustering storm, which accompanied it, bowed down the trees and bushes around them like dry reeds and threw them beyond. Rudy lay cast on the earth; the trunk of the tree on which he had held was as though sawed off, and its crown was hurled still farther along. His uncle lay amongst the broken branches, with his head shattered; his hands were yet warm, but his face was no longer to be recognized. Rudy stood pale and trembling; this was the first terror of his life, the first hour of fear that he had ever known.

Late in the evening, he returned with his message of death to his home, which was now one of sorrow.

The wife stood without words, without tears, and not until the corpse was brought home did her sorrow find an outburst. The poor cretin crept to his bed and was not seen all day, but towards evening he came to Rudy, and said: "Write a letter for me. Saperli cannot write! Saperli can take the letter to the post office."

"A letter for you," asked Rudy, "and to whom?"

"To our Lord Christ!"

"What do you mean?"

And the half-witted creature gave a touching glance at Rudy, folded his hands and said piously and solemnly:

"Jesus Christ! Saperli wishes to send him a letter, praying him to let Saperli lie dead and not the man of this house!"

And Rudy pressed his hand, "the letter cannot be sent, the letter will not give him back to us!"

It was difficult for Rudy to explain the impossibility to him.

"Now you are the stay of the house!" said his foster-mother, and Rudy became it.

Babette

Who is the best shot in Canton Valais? The chamois knew only too well: "Beware of Rudy!" they could say. Who is the handsomest hunter?—"It is Rudy." The young girls said this also, but they did not say: "Beware of Rudy!" No, not even the grave mothers, for he nodded to them quite as amicably as to the young girls. He was so bold and gay, his cheeks were brown, his teeth fresh and white and his coal-black eyes glittered; he was a handsome young fellow and but twenty years old. The icy water did not sting him when he swam, he could turn around in it like a fish; he could climb as did no one, and he was as firm on the rocky walls as a snail—for he had good sinews and muscles that served him well in leaping—the cat had first taught him this, and later the chamois. One could not trust one's self to a better guide than to Rudy. In this way he could collect quite a fortune, but he had no taste for the trade of a cooper, which his uncle had taught him; his delight and pleasure was to shoot chamois, and this was profitable also. Rudy was a good match if one did not look higher than one's station, and in dancing he was just the kind of dancer that young girls dream about, and one or the other were always thinking of him when they were awake.

"He kissed me whilst dancing!" said the schoolmaster's Annette to her most intimate friend, but she should not have said this, not even to her dearest friend, but it is difficult to keep such things to one's self—like sand in a purse with a hole in it, it soon runs out—and although Rudy was so steady and good it was soon known that he kissed whilst dancing.

"Watch him," said an old hunter, "he has commenced with A, and he will kiss the whole alphabet through!"

A kiss, at a dance, was all they could say in their gossiping, but he had kissed Annette, and she was by no means the flower of his heart.

Down near Bex, between the great walnut trees, close by a rapid little stream, dwelt the rich miller. The dwelling-house was a large three-storied building, with little towers covered with wood and coated with sheets of lead, which shone in the sunshine and in the moonshine; the largest tower had for a weather-cock a bright arrow which pierced an apple and which was intended to represent the apple shot by Tell. The mill looked neat and comfortable, so that it was really worth describing and drawing, but the miller's daughter could neither be described nor drawn, at least so said Rudy. Yet she was imprinted in his heart, and her eyes acted as a fire-brand upon it, and this had happened suddenly and unexpectedly. The most wonderful part of all was, that the miller's daughter, the pretty Babette, thought not of him, for she and Rudy had never even spoken two words with each other.

The miller was rich, and riches placed her much too high to be approached; "but no one," said Rudy to himself, "is placed so high as to be unapproachable; one must climb and one does not fall, when one does not think of it." This knowledge he had brought from home with him.

Now it so happened that Rudy had business at Bex and it was quite a journey there, for the railroad was not completed. The broad valley of Valais stretches itself from the glaciers of the Rhone, under the foot of the Simplon-mountain, between many varying mountain-heights, with its mighty river, the Rhone, which often swells and destroys everything, overflooding fields and roads. The valley makes a bend, between the towns of Sion and St. Maurice, like an elbow and becomes so narrow at Maurice, that there only remains sufficient room for the river bed and a cart way. Here an old tower stands like a sentry before the Canton Valais; it ends at this point and overlooks the bridge, which has a wall towards the custom-house. Now begins the Canton called Pays de Vaud and the nearest town is Bex, where everything becomes luxuriant and fruitful—one is in a garden of walnut and chestnut trees and here and there, cypress and pomegranate blossoms peep out—it is as warm as the South; one imagines one's self transplanted into Italy.

Rudy reached Bex, accomplished his business and looked about him, but he did not see a single miller's boy, not to speak of Babette. It appeared as though they were not to meet.

It was evening, the air was heavy with the wild thyme and blooming linden, a glistening veil lay over the forest-clad mountains, there was a stillness over everything, but not the quiet of sleep. It seemed as though all nature retained her breath, as if she felt disposed to allow her image to be imprinted upon the firmament.

Here and there, there were poles standing on the green fields, between the trees; they held the telegraph wire, which has been conducted through this peaceful valley. An object leant against one of these poles, so immoveable, that one might have taken it for a withered trunk of a tree; but it was Rudy. He slept not and still less was he dead; but as the most important events of this earth, as well as affairs of vital moment for individuals pass over the wires, without their giving out a tone or a tremulous movement, even so flashed through Rudy, thoughts—powerful, overwhelming, speaking of the happiness of his life; his, henceforth, "constant thought." His eyes were fixed upon a point in the trellis-work, and this was a light in Babette's sitting room. Rudy was so motionless, one might have thought that he was observing a chamois, in order to shoot it. Now, however, he was like the chamois—which appears sculptured on the rock, and suddenly if a stone rolls, springs and flies away—thus stood Rudy, until a thought struck him.

"Never despair," said he. "I shall make a visit to the mill, and say: Good evening miller, good evening Babette! One does not fall when one does not think of it! Babette must see me, if I am to be her husband!"

And Rudy laughed, was of good cheer and went to the mill; he knew what he wanted, he wanted Babette.

The river, with its yellowish white water rolled on; the willow trees and the lindens bowed themselves deep in the hastening water; Rudy went along the path, and as it says in the old child's song:

—— —— —— Zu des Müllers Haus,
Aber da war Niemand drinnen
Nur die Katze schaute aus!*

*The cat looked out from the miller's house,
No one was in, not even a mouse!

The house-cat stood on the step, put up her back and said: "Miau!" but Rudy had no thoughts for her language, he knocked, no one heard, no one opened. "Miau!" said the cat. If Rudy had been little, he would have understood the speech of animals and known that the cat told him: "There is no one at home!" He was obliged to cross over to the mill, to make inquiries, and here he had news. The master of the house was away on a journey, far away in the town of Interlaken—inter lacus, "between the lakes"—as the school-master, Annette's father, had explained, in his wisdom. Far away was the miller and Babette with him; there was to be a shooting festival, which was to commence on the following day and to continue for a whole week. The Swiss from all the German cantons were to meet there.

Poor Rudy, one could well say that he had not taken the happiest time to visit Bex; now he could return and that was what he did. He took the road over Sion and St. Maurice, back to his own valley, back to his own mountain, but he was not down-cast. On the following morning, when the sun rose, his good humour had returned, in fact it had never left him.

"Babette is in Interlaken, many a day's journey from here!" said he to himself, "it is a long road thither, if one goes by the highway, but not so far if one passes over the rocks and that is the road for a chamois hunter! I went this road formerly, for there is my home, where I lived with my grandfather when I was a little child, and they have a shooting festival in Interlaken! I will be the first one there, and that will I be with Babette also, as soon as I have made her acquaintance!"

With his light knapsack containing his Sunday clothes, with his gun and his huntsman's pouch, Rudy ascended the mountain. The short road, was a pretty long one, but the shooting-match had but commenced to-day and was to last more than a week; the miller and Babette were to remain the whole time, with their relations in Interlaken. Rudy crossed the Gemmi, for he wished to go to Grindel-wald.

He stepped forwards merry and well, out into the fresh, light mountain air. The valley sank beneath him, the horizon widened; here and there a snow-peak, and soon appeared the whole shining white alpine chain. Rudy knew every snow mountain, onward he strode towards the Schreckhorn, that elevates its white powdered snow-finger high in the air.

At last he crossed the ridge of the mountain and the pasture-grounds and reached the valley of his home; the air was light and his spirits gay, mountain and valley stood resplendent with verdure and flowers. His heart was filled with youthful thoughts;—that one can never grow old, never die; but live, rule and enjoy;—free as a bird, light as a bird was he. The swallows flew by and sang as in his childhood: "We and you, and You and we!" All was happiness.

Below lay the velvet-green meadow, with its brown wooden houses, the Lütschine hummed and roared. He saw the glacier with its green glass edges and its black crevices in the deep snow, and the under and upper glacier. The sound of the church-bells was carried over to him, as if they chimed a welcome home; his heart beat loudly and expanded, so, that for a moment, Babette vanished from it; his heart widened, it was so full of recollections. He retraced his steps, over the path, where he used to stand when a little boy, with the other children, on the edge of the ditch, and where he sold carved wooden houses. Yonder, under the fir-trees was his grandfather's house,—strangers dwelled there. Children came running up the path, wishing to sell; one of them held an alpine rose towards him. Rudy took it for a good omen and thought of Babette. Quickly he crossed the bridge, where the two Lütschines meet; the leafy trees had increased and the walnut trees gave deeper shade. He saw the streaming Swiss and Danish flags—the white cross on the red cloth—and Interlaken lay before him.

It was certainly a magnificent town; like no other, it seemed to Rudy. A Swiss town in its Sunday dress, was not like other trading-places, a mass of black stone houses, heavy, uninviting and stiff. No! it looked as though the wooden houses, on the mountain had run down into the green valley, to the clear, swift river and had ranged themselves in a row—a little in and out—so as to form a street, the most splendid of all streets, which had grown up since Rudy was here as a child. It appeared to him, that here all the pretty wooden houses that his grandfather had carved, and with which the cup-board at home used to be filled, had placed themselves there and had grown in strength, as the old, the oldest chestnut trees had done. Each house had carved wood-work around the windows and balconies, projecting roofs, pretty and neat; in front of every house a little flower garden extended into the stone-covered street. The houses were all placed on one side, as if they wished to conceal the forest-green meadow, where the cows with their tinkling bells made one fancy one's self near the high alpine pasture-grounds. The meadow was enclosed with high mountains, that leaned to one side so that the Jungfrau, the most stately of the Swiss mountains, with its glistening snow-clad top, was visible.

What a quantity of well dressed ladies and gentlemen from foreign countries! What multitudes of inhabitants from the different cantons! The shooters, with their numbers placed in a wreath around their hats, waiting to take their turn. Here was music and song, hurdy-gurdys and wind instruments, cries and confusion. The houses and bridges were decked with devices and verses; banners and flags floated, rifles sounded shot after shot; this was the best music to Rudy's ear and he entirely forgot Babette, although he had come for her sake.

The marksmen thronged towards the spot where the target-shooting was; Rudy was soon among them and he was the best, the luckiest, for he always hit the mark.

"Who can the strange hunter be?" they asked, "He speaks the French language as though he came from Canton Valais!" "He speaks our German very distinctly!" said others. "He is said to have lived in the neighbourhood of Grindelwald, when a child!" said one of them.

There was life in the youth; his eyes sparkled, his aim was true. Good luck gives courage, and Rudy had courage at all times; he soon had a large circle of friends around him, they praised him, they did homage to him, and Babette had almost entirely left his thoughts. At that moment a heavy hand struck him on the shoulder, and a gruff voice addressed him in the French tongue:

"You are from Canton Valais?"

Rudy turned around. A stout person, with a red, contented countenance, stood by him and that was the rich miller of Bex. He covered with his wide body, the slight pretty Babette, who however, soon peeped out with her beaming dark eyes. The rich peasant became consequential because the hunter from his canton had made the best shot and was the honoured one. Rudy was certainly a favourite of fortune, that, for which he had journeyed thither and almost forgotten had sought him.

When one meets a countryman far from one's home, why then one knows one another, and speaks together. Rudy was the first at the shooting festival and the miller was the first at Bex, through his money and mill, and so the two men pressed each other's hands: this they had never done before. Babette also, gave Rudy her little hand and he pressed her's in return and looked at her, so—that she became quite red.

The miller told of the long journey which they had made here, of the many large towns which they had seen—that was a real journey; they had come in the steam-boat and had been driven by post and rail!

"I came by the short road," said Rudy, "I came over the mountains; there is no path so high, that one can not reach it!"

"But one can break one's neck," said the miller, "you look as though you would do so some day, you are so daring!"

"One does not fall, when one does not think of it!" said Rudy.

And the miller's family in Interlaken, with whom the miller and Babette were staying, begged Rudy to pay them a visit, for he was from the same canton as their relations.

These were glad tidings for Rudy, fortune smiled upon him, as it always does on those that rely upon themselves and think upon the saying: "Our Lord gives us nuts, but he does not crack them for us!" Rudy made himself quite at home with the miller's relations; they drank the health of the best marksman. Babette knocked her glass against his and Rudy gave thanks for the honour shown him.

In the evening, they all walked under the walnut trees, in front of the decorated hôtels; there was such a crowd, such a throng, that Rudy was obliged to offer his arm to Babette. "He was so rejoiced to have met people from Pays de Vaud," said he, "Pays de Vaud and Valais were good neighbourly cantons." His joy was so profound that it struck Babette, she must press his hand. They walked along almost like old acquaintances; she was so amusing, the darling little creature, it became her so prettily Rudy thought, when she described what was laughable and overdone in the dress of the ladies, and ridiculed their manners and walk. She did not do this in order to mock them, for no doubt they were very good people, yes! kind and amiable. Babette knew what was right, for she had a god-mother that was a distinguished English lady. She was in Bex, eighteen years ago, when Babette was baptized; she had given Babette, the expensive breastpin which she wore. The god-mother had written her two letters; this year she was to meet her in Interlaken, with her daughters; they were old maids, over thirty years old, said Babette;—she was just eighteen.

The sweet little mouth was not still a minute; everything that Babette said, sounded to Rudy of great importance. Then he related how often he had been in Bex, how well he knew the mill; how often he had seen Babette, but she of course had never remarked him; he told how, when he reached the mill, with many thoughts to which he could give no utterance, she and her father were far away; still not so far as to render it impossible for him to ascend the rocky wall which made the road so long.

Yes, he said this; and he also said how much he thought of her; that it was for her sake and not on account of the shooting festival that he had come.

Babette remained very still, for what he confided to her was almost too much joy.

The sun set behind the rocky wall, whilst they were walking, and there stood the Jungfrau in all her radiant splendour, surrounded by the dark green circle of the adjacent mountains. The vast crowd of people stopped to look at it, Rudy and Babette also gazed upon its grandeur.

"It is nowhere more beautiful than here!" said Babette.

"Nowhere!" said Rudy, and looked at Babette.

"I must leave to-morrow!" said he, a little later.

"Visit us in Bex," whispered Babette, "it will delight my father!"

Homewards

Ah! how much Rudy carried with him, as he went home the next morning over the mountains. Yes, there were three silver goblets, two very fine rifles and a silver coffee pot, which one could use if one wished to go to house-keeping; but he carried with him something far, far more important, far mightier, or rather that carried him over the high mountains.

The weather was raw, moist and cold, grey and heavy; the clouds lowered over the mountain-tops like mourning veils, and enveloped the shining peaks of the rocks. The sound of the axe resounded from the depths of the forest, and the trunks of the trees rolled down the mountain, looking in the distance like slight sticks, but on approaching them they were heavy trees, suitable for making masts. The Lütschine rushed on with its monotonous sound, the wind blustered, the clouds sailed by.

Suddenly a young girl approached Rudy, whom he had not noticed before; not until she was beside him; she also was about crossing the mountain. Her eyes had so peculiar a power that one was forced to look into them; they were so strangely clear—clear as glass, so deep, so fathomless—

"Have you a beloved one?" asked Rudy; for to have a beloved one was everything to him.

"I have none!" said she, and laughed; but it was as though she was not speaking the truth. "Do not let us take a by-way," continued she, "we must go more to the left, that way is shorter!"

"Yes, so as to fall down a precipice!" said Rudy; "Do you know no better way, and yet wish to be a guide?"

"I know the road well," said she, "my thoughts are

with me; yours are beneath in the valley; here on high, one must think on the Ice-Maiden, for they say she is not well disposed to mankind!"

"I do not fear her," said Rudy, "she was forced to let me go when I was a child, so I suppose I can slip away from her now that I am older!"

The darkness increased, the rain fell, the snow came; it shone and dazzled. "Give me your hand, I will help you to ascend!" said the girl, and touched him with icy-cold fingers.

"You help me," said Rudy, "I do not yet need a woman's help in climbing!" He strode quickly on, away from her; the snow-shower formed a curtain around him, the wind whistled by him and he heard the young girl laugh and sing; it sounded so oddly! Yes, that was certainly a spirit in the service of the Ice-Maiden. Rudy had heard of them, when he had passed a night on high; when he had crossed the mountain, as a little boy.

The snow fell more scantily and the shadows lay under him; he looked back, there was no one to be seen, but he heard laughing and jodling and it did not appear to come from a human being. When Rudy reached the uppermost portion of the mountain, where the rocky path leads to the valley of the Rhone, he saw in the direction of Chamouni, two bright stars, twinkling and shining in the clear streaks of blue; he thought of Babette, of himself, of his happiness and became warmed by his thoughts.

The Visit to the Mill

"You bring princely things into the house!" said the old foster-mother, her singular eagle-eyes glistened and she made strange and hasty motions with her lean neck.

"Fortune is with you, Rudy, I must kiss you, my sweet boy!"

Rudy allowed himself to be kissed, but one could read in his countenance, that he but submitted to circumstances and to little household miseries. "How handsome you are, Rudy!" said the old woman.

"Do not put notions into my head!" answered Rudy, and laughed, but still it pleased him.

"I say it once more," said the old woman, "fortune is with you!"

"Yes, I agree with you there!" said he; thought of Babette and longed to be in the deep valley. "They must have returned, two days have passed since they expected to do so. I must go to Bex!"

Rudy went to Bex, and the inhabitants of the mill had returned; he was well received and they brought him greetings from the family at Interlaken. Babette did not talk much, she had grown silent; but her eyes spoke and that was quite enough for Rudy. The miller who generally liked to carry on the conversation—for he was accustomed to have every one laugh at his witty sayings and puns— was he not the rich miller?—seemed now to prefer to listen. Rudy recounted to him his hunting expeditions; described the difficulties, the dangers and the privations of the chamois hunter when on the lofty mountain peak; how often he must climb over the insecure snow-ledges, that the wind had blown on the rocky brink, and how he must pass over slight bridges that the snow-drifts had thrown across the abyss. Rudy looked fearless, his eyes sparkled whilst he spoke of the shrewdness of the chamois, of their daring leaps, of the violence of the Föhn and of the rolling avalanches. He observed that with every description he won more and more favour; but what pleased the miller more than all, was the account of the lamb's vulture and the bold golden eagle.

In Canton Valais, not far from here, there was an eagle's nest, very slyly built under the projecting edge of the rock; a young one was in it, but no one could steal it! An Englishman had offered Rudy a few days before, a whole handful of gold, if he would bring him the young one alive, "but everything has a limit," said he, "the young eagle cannot be taken away, and it would be madness to attempt it!"

The wine and conversation flowed freely; but the evening appeared all too short for Rudy; yet it was past midnight, when he went home from his first visit to the mill.

The light shone a little while longer through the window and between the green trees; the parlour-cat came out of an opening in the roof and the kitchen-cat came along the gutter.

"Do you know the latest news at the mill?" said the parlour-cat, "there has been a silent betrothal in the house!

Father does not yet know it, but Rudy and Babette have reached each other their paws under the table, and he trod three times on my fore-paws, but still I did not mew, for that would have awakened attention!"

"I should have done it, nevertheless!" said the kitchen-cat.

"What is suited to the kitchen is not suited to the parlour," said the parlour-cat. "I should like to know what the miller will say, when he hears of the betrothal!"

Yes, what the miller would say! That was what Rudy would have liked to know, for Rudy was not at all patient. When the omnibus rumbled over the bridge of the Rhone, between Valais and Pays de Vaud not many days after, Rudy sat in it and was of good cheer; filled with pleasing thoughts of the "Yes," of the same evening.

When evening came and the omnibus returned, yes, there sat Rudy within, but the parlour-cat, was running about in the mill with great news.

"Listen, you, in the kitchen! The miller knows everything now. This has had an exquisite ending! Rudy came here towards evening; he and Babette had much to whisper and to chatter about, as they stood in the walk, under the miller's chamber. I lay close to their feet but they had neither eyes nor thoughts for me. 'I am going directly to your father,' said Rudy, 'this is an honourable affair!' 'Shall I follow you?' asked Babette, 'it may give you more courage!' 'I have courage enough,' said Rudy, 'but if you are there, he will be forced to look at it in a more favourable light!' They went in. Rudy trod heavily on my tail! Rudy is indescribably awkward; I mewed, but neither he nor Babette had ears to hear it. They opened the door, they entered and I preceded them; I leaped upon the back of a chair, for I did not know but that Rudy would overturn everything! But the miller reversed all, that was a great step! Out of the door, up the mountains, to the chamois! Rudy can aim at them now, but not at our little Babette!"

"But what was said?" asked the kitchen-cat.

"Said? Everything. 'I care for her and she cares for me! When there is milk enough in the jug for one, there is milk enough in the jug for two!' 'But she is placed too high for you,' said the miller, 'she sits on gold dust, so now you know it; you can not reach her!' 'Nothing is too high; he who wills can reach anything!' said Rudy. He is too headstrong on this subject! 'But you cannot reach the eaglet, you said so yourself lately! Babette is still higher!' 'I will have them both!' said Rudy. 'Yes, I will bestow her upon you, if you make me a present of the eaglet alive!' said the miller and laughed until the tears stood in his eyes.

"'Thanks for your visit, Rudy! Come again to-morrow, you will find no one at home. Farewell, Rudy!' Babette said farewell also, as sorrowfully as a kitten, that cannot see its mother. 'A word is a word, a man is a man,' said Rudy, 'do not weep Babette, I shall bring the eaglet!' 'I hope that you will break your neck!' said the miller. That's what I call an overturning! Now Rudy has gone, and Babette sits and weeps; but the miller sings in German, he learned to do so whilst on his journey! I do not intend to trouble myself any longer about it, it does no good!"

"There is still a prospect!" said the kitchen-cat.

The Eagle's Nest

Merry and loud sounded the jodel from the mountain-path, it indicated good humour and joyous courage; it was Rudy; he was going to his friend Vesinand.

"You must help me! We will take Ragli with us; I am going after the eaglet on the brink of the rock!"

"Do you not wish to go after the black spot in the moon? That is quite as easy," said Vesinand; "you are in a good humour!"

"Yes, because I am thinking of my wedding; but seriously, you shall know how my affairs stand!"

Vesinand and Ragli soon knew what Rudy wished.

"You are a bold fellow," said they, "do not do this! You will break your neck!"

"One does not fall, when one does not think of it!" said Rudy.

About mid-day, they set out with poles, ladders and ropes; their path lay through bushes and brambles, over the rolling stones, up, up in the dark night.

The water rushed beneath them; the water flowed above them and the humid clouds chased each other in the air. The hunters approached the steep brink of the rock; it became darker and darker, the rocky walls almost met; high above them in the narrow fissure the air penetrated and gave light. Under their feet there was a deep abyss with its roaring waters.

They all three sat still, awaiting the grey of the morning; then the eagle would fly out; they must shoot him before they could think of obtaining the young one. Rudy seemed to be a part of the stone on which he sat; his rifle placed before him, ready to take aim, his eyes immoveably fastened on yon high cleft which concealed the eagle's nest. The three huntsmen waited long.

A crashing, whizzing noise sounded high above them; a large hovering object darkened the air. Two rifle barrels were aimed as the black eagle flew from its nest; a shot was heard, the out-spread wings moved an instant, then the bird slowly sank as if it wished to fill the entire cliff with its outstretched wings and bury the huntsmen in its fall. The eagle sank in the deep; the branches of the trees and bushes cracked, broken by the fall of the bird.

They now displayed their activity; three of the longest ladders were tied together; they stood them on the farthest point where the foot could place itself with security, close to the brink of the precipice—but they were not long enough; there was still a great space from the outermost projecting cliff, which protected the nest; the rocky wall was perfectly smooth. After some consultation, they decided to lower into the opening two ladders tied together and to fasten them to the three already beneath them. With great difficulty they dragged them up and attached them with cords; the ladders shot over the projecting cliffs and hung over the chasm; Rudy sat already on the lowest round.

It was an ice-cold morning, and the mist mounted from the black ravine. Rudy sat there like a fly on a rocking blade of grass, which a nest-building bird has dropped in its hasty flight, on the edge of a factory chimney; but the fly had the advantage of escaping by its wings, poor Rudy had none, he was almost sure to break his neck. The wind whistled around him and the roaring water from the thawed glaciers, the palace of the Ice-Maiden, poured itself into the abyss.

He gave the ladders a swinging motion—as the spider swings herself by her long thread—he seized them with a strong and steady hand, but they shook as if they had worn-out hasps.

The five long ladders looked like a tremulous reed, as they reached the nest and hung perpendicularly over the rocky wall. Now came the most dangerous part; Rudy had to climb as a cat climbs; but Rudy could do this, for the cat had taught it to him. He did not feel that Vertigo trod in the air behind him and stretched her polypus-like arms towards him. Now he stood on the highest round of the ladder and perceived that he was not sufficiently high to enable him to see into the nest; he could reach it with his hands. He tried how firm the twigs were, which plaited in one another formed the bottom of the nest; when he had assured himself of a thick and immoveable one, he swung himself off of the ladder. He had his breast and head over the nest, out of which streamed towards him a stifling stench of carrion; torn lambs, chamois and birds lay decomposing around him. Vertigo, who had no power over him, blew poisonous vapours into his face to stupify him; below in the black, yawning abyss, sat the Ice-Maiden herself, on the hastening water, with her long greenish-white hair and stared at him with death-like eyes, which were pointed at him like two rifle barrels.

"Now, I shall catch you!"

Seated in one corner of the eagle's nest was the eaglet, who could not fly yet, although so strong and powerful. Rudy fastened his eyes on it, held himself with his whole strength firmly by one hand, and with the other threw the noose around it. It was captured alive, its legs were in the knot; Rudy cast the rope over his shoulder, so that the animal dangled some distance below him, and sustained himself by another rope which hung down, until his feet touched the upper round of the ladder.

"Hold fast, do not think that you will fall and then you are sure not to do so!" That was the old lesson, and he followed it; held fast, climbed, was sure not to fall and he did not.

There resounded a strong jodling, and a joyous one too. Rudy stood on the firm, rocky ground with the young eaglet.

The News Which the Parlour-Cat Related

"Here is what you demanded!" said Rudy, on entering the house of the miller at Bex, as he placed a large basket on the floor and took off the covering. Two yellow eyes, with black circles around them, fiery and wild, looked out as if they wished to set on fire, or to kill those around them. The short beak yawned ready to bite and the neck was red and downy.

"The eaglet!" cried the miller. Babette screamed, jumped to one side and could neither turn her eyes from Rudy, nor from the eaglet.

"You do not allow yourself to be frightened!" said the miller.

"And you keep your word, at all times," said Rudy, "each has his characteristic trait!"

"But why did you not break your neck?" asked the miller.

"Because I held on firmly," answered Rudy, "and I hold firmly on Babette!"

"First see that you have her!" said the miller and laughed; that was a good sign; Babette knew this.

"Let us take the eaglet from the basket, it is terrible to see how he glares! How did you get him?"

Rudy was obliged to recount his adventure, whilst the miller stared at him with eyes, which grew larger and larger.

"With your courage and with your luck you could take care of three wives!" said the miller.

"Thanks! Thanks!" cried Rudy.

"Yes, but you have not yet Babette!" said the miller as he struck the young chamois hunter, jestingly on the shoulder.

"Do you know the latest news in the mill?" said the parlour-cat to the kitchen-cat. "Rudy has brought us the young eagle and taken Babette in exchange. They have kissed each other and the father looked on. That is just as good as a betrothal; the old man did not overturn anything, he drew in his claws, took his nap and left the two seated, caressing each other. They have so much to relate, they will not get through till Christmas!"

They had not finished at Christmas.

The wind whistled through the brown foliage, the snow swept through the valley as it did on the high mountains. The Ice-Maiden sat in her proud castle and arrayed herself in her winter costume; the ice walls stood in glazed frost; where the mountain streams waved their watery veil in summer, were now seen thick elephantine icicles, shining garlands of ice, formed of fantastic ice crystals, encircled the fir-trees, which were powdered with snow.

The Ice-Maiden rode on the blustering wind over the deepest valleys. The snow covering lay over all Bex; Rudy stayed in doors more than was his wont, and sat with Babette. The wedding was to take place in the summer; their friends talked so much of it that it often made their ears burn. All was sunshine with them, and the loveliest alpine rose was Babette, the sprightly, laughing Babette, who was as charming as the early spring; the spring that makes the birds sing, that will bring the summer time and the wedding day.

"How can they sit there and hang over each other," exclaimed the parlour-cat, "I am really tired of their eternal mewing!"

The Ice-Maiden

The early spring time had unfolded the green leaves of the walnut and chestnut trees; they were remarkably luxuriant from the bridge of St. Maurice to the banks of the lake of Geneva.

The Rhone, which rushes forth from its source, has under the green glacier the palace of the Ice-Maiden. She is carried by it and the sharp wind to the elevated snow-fields, where she extends herself on her damp cushions in the brilliant sunshine. There she sits and gazes, with far-seeing sight, upon the valley where mortals busily move about like so many ants.

"Beings endowed with mental powers, as the children of the Sun, call you," said the Ice-Maiden—"ye are worms! One snow-ball rolled and you and your houses and towns are crushed and swept away!" She raised her proud head still higher and looked with death-beaming eyes far around and below her. From the valley resounded a rumbling, a blasting of rocks, men were making railways and tunnels. "They are playing like moles," said she, "they excavate passages, and a noise is made like the firing of a gun. When I transpose my castles, it roars louder than the rolling of the thunder!"

A smoke arose from the valley and moved along like a floating veil, like a waving plume; it was the locomotive which led the train over the newly built railroad—this crooked snake, whose limbs are formed of cars upon cars. It shot along with the speed of an arrow.

"They are playing the masters with their mental powers," said the Ice-Maiden, "but the powers of nature are the ruling ones!" and she laughed and her laugh was echoed in the valley.

"Now an avalanche is rolling!" said the men below.

Still more loudly sang the children of the Sun; they sang of the "thoughts" of men which fetter the sea to the yoke, cut down mountains and fill up valleys; of human thoughts which rule the powers of nature. At this moment, a company of travellers crossed the snow-field where the Maiden sat; they had bound themselves firmly together with ropes, in order to form a large body on the smooth ice-field by the deep abyss.

"Worms!" said she, "as if you were lords of creation!" She turned from them and looked mockingly upon the deep valley, where the cars were rushing by.

"There sit those thoughts in their power of strength! I see them all!—There sits one, proud as a king and alone! They sit in masses! There, half are asleep! When the steam-dragon stops, they will descend and go their way! The thoughts go out into the world!" She laughed.

"There rolls another avalanche!" they said in the valley.

"It will not catch us!" said two on the back of the steam dragon;—"two souls and one thought"—these were Rudy and Babette; the miller was there also.

"As baggage," said he, "I go along, as the indispensable!"

"There sit the two," said the Ice-Maiden, "I have crushed many a chamois; I have bent and broken millions of alpine roses, so that no roots were left! I shall annihilate them! The thoughts! The mental powers!" She laughed.

"There rolls another avalanche!" they said in the valley.

The God-Mother

In Montreux, one of the adjoining towns, which with Clarens, Vernex and Crin forms a garland around the northeast part of the lake of Geneva, dwelt Babette's god-mother, a distinguished English lady, with her daughters and a young relation. Although she had but lately arrived, the miller had already made her his visit and announced Babette's engagement; had spoken of Rudy and the eaglet; of the visit to Interlaken and in short had told the whole story. This had rejoiced her in the highest degree, both for Rudy and Babette's sake, as well as for the miller's; they must all visit her—therefore they came. Babette was to see her god-mother, and the god-mother was to see Babette.

At the end of the lake of Geneva, by the little town of Villeneuve, lay the steam-boat which after half an hour's trip from Vernex, arrived at Montreux. This is one of the coasts which are sung of by the poets. Here sat Byron, by the deep bluish green lake, under the walnut trees and wrote his melodious verses upon the prisoner of the deep sombre castle of Chillon. Here, where Clarens with its weeping willows, mirrored itself in the waters, once wandered Rousseau and dreamt of Heloïse. Yonder, where the Rhone glides along under Savoy's snow-topped mountains and not far from its mouth, in the lake lies a little island, indeed it is so small, that from the coast it is taken for a vessel. It is a valley between the rocks, which a lady caused to be dammed up a hundred years ago and to be covered with earth and planted with three acacia-trees, which now shade the whole island. Babette was quite charmed with this little spot; they must and should go there, yes, it must be charming beyond description to be on the island; but the steamer sailed by, and stopped as it should, at Vernex.

The little party wandered between the white, sunlighted walls, which surround the vineyards of the little mountain town of Montreux, through the fig-trees which flourish before every peasant's house and in whose gardens, the laurel and cypress trees are green. Half-way up the hill stood the boarding house where the god-mother resided.

The reception was very cordial. The god-mother was a large amiable person and had a round smiling countenance; as a child she must have had a real Raphael's angel head, but now it was an old angel's head with silvery white hair, well curled. The daughters were tall, slender, refined and much dressed. The young cousin who was with them, was clad in white from head to foot; he had golden hair and immense whiskers; he immediately showed little Babette the greatest attention.

Richly bound books, loose music and drawings lay strewn about the large table; the balcony door stood open and one had a view of the beautiful out-spread lake, which was so shining, so still, that the mountains of Savoy with their little villages, their forest and their snowy peaks mirrored themselves in it.

Rudy, who usually was so full of life, so merry and so daring, did not feel in his element; he moved about over the smooth floor as though he were treading on peas. How wearily the time dragged along, it was just as if one was in a tread mill! If they did go walking, why, that was just as slow; Rudy could take two steps forwards and two steps backwards and still remain in the pace of the others.

When they came to Chillon, (the old sombre castle on the rocky island) they entered in order to see the dungeon and the martyr's stake, as well as the rusty chains on the wall; the stone bed for those condemned to death and the trap-door where the wretched beings impaled on iron goads, were hurled into the breakers. It was a place of execution elevated through Byron's song to the world of poetry. Rudy was sad, he lent over the broad stone sill of the window, gazed into the deep blue water and over to the little solitary island with its three acacias and wished himself there, free from the whole gossiping society. Babette was remarkably merry, she had been indescribably amused. The cousin found her perfect.

"Yes, a perfect jackanapes!" said Rudy; this was the first time, that he had said something, that did not please her. The Englishman had presented her with a little book, as a souvenir of Chillon,—Byron's poem of "The Prisoner of Chillon," in the French language, so that Babette might read it.

"The book may be good," said Rudy, "but the finely combed fellow that gave it to you does not please me!"

"He looked like a meal-bag, without meal in it!" said the miller and laughed at his own wit. Rudy laughed and thought that this was very well said.

The Cousin

When Rudy came to the mill, a couple of days afterwards, he found the young Englishman there. Babette had just cooked some trout for him and had dressed them with parsley in order to make them appear more inviting. That was assuredly not necessary. What did the Englishman want here? Did he come in order to have Babette entertain and wait upon him?

Rudy was jealous and that amused Babette; it rejoiced her, to learn the feelings of his heart, the strong as well as the weak ones.

Until now love had been a play and she played with Rudy's whole heart; yet he was her happiness, her life's thought, the noblest one! The more gloomy he looked, the more her eyes laughed and she would have liked to kiss the blonde Englishman with his golden whiskers, if she could have succeeded by so doing, in making Rudy rush away furious. Then, yes then, she would have known how much he loved her. That was not right, that was not wise in little Babette; but she was only nineteen! She did not reflect and still less did she think how her behaviour towards the young Englishman might be interpreted; for it was lighter and merrier than was seemly for the honourable and newly affianced daughter of the miller.

The mill lay where the highway slopes—under the snow covered rocky heights—which are called here, in the language of the country "Diablerets" close to a rapid mountain stream, which was of a greyish white, like bubbling soap suds. A smaller stream, rushes forth from the rocks on the other side of the river, passes through an enclosed, broad rafter-made-gutter and turns the large wheel of the mill. The gutter was so full of water, that it streamed over and offered a most slippery way, to one who had the idea of crossing more quickly to the mill; a young man had this idea—the Englishman. Guided by the light, which shone from Babette's window, he arrived in the evening, clothed in white, like a miller's boy; he had not learnt to climb and nearly tumbled head over heels into the stream, but escaped with wet sleeves and splashed pantaloons. He reached Babette's window, muddy and wet through, there he climbed into the old linden tree and imitated the screech of an owl, for he could not sing like any other bird. Babette heard it and peeped through the thin curtains, but when she remarked the white man and recognized him, her little heart fluttered with alarm, but also with anger. She hastily extinguished the light, fastened the windows securely and then she let him howl.

If Rudy was in the mill it would have been dreadful, but Rudy was not there; no, it was much worse, for he was below. There was loud conversation, angry words; there might be blows; yes, perhaps murder.

Babette was terrified; she opened the window, called Rudy's name and begged him to go; she said she would not suffer him to remain.

"You will not suffer me to remain," he exclaimed, "then it is a preconcerted thing! You were expecting other friends, friends better than myself; shame on you, Babette!"

"You are detestable," said Babette, "I hate you!" and she wept. "Go! Go!"

"I have not deserved this!" said he, and departed. His cheeks burned like fire, his heart burned like fire.

Babette threw herself on her bed and wept.

"So much as I love you, Rudy, how can you believe ill of me!"

She was angry, very angry, and this was good for her; otherwise she would have sorrowed deeply; but now she could sleep, and she slept the strengthening sleep of youth.

The Evil Powers

Rudy forsook Bex and went on his way home, in the fresh, cool air, up the snow-covered mountain, where the Ice-Maiden ruled. The leafy trees which lay beneath him, looked like potato vines; fir-trees and bushes became less frequent; the alpine roses grew in the snow, which lay in little spots like linen put out to bleach. There stood a blue anemone, he crushed it with the barrel of his gun.

Higher up two chamois appeared and Rudy's eyes gained lustre and his thoughts took a new direction; but he was not near enough to make a good shot; he ascended still higher, where only stiff grass grows between the blocks of stone; the chamois were quietly crossing the snow field; he hurried hastily on; the fog was descending and he suddenly stood before the steep rocky wall. The rain commenced to fall.

He felt a burning thirst; heat in his head, cold in all his limbs; he grasped his hunting flask, but it was empty; he had not thought of filling it when he rushed up the hill. He had never been ill, but now he was so; he was weary and had a desire to throw himself down to sleep, but everything was streaming with water. He endeavoured to collect his ideas, but all objects danced before his eyes. Suddenly he perceived a newly built house leaning against the rocks and in the doorway stood a young girl. Yes, it appeared to him that it was the schoolmaster's Annette, whom he had once kissed whilst dancing; but it was not Annette and yet he had seen her before—perhaps in Grindelwald, on the evening when he returned from the shooting-festival at Interlaken.

"Where do you come from?" asked he.

"I am at home," said she, "I tend my flock!"

"Your flock, where do they pasture? Here are only cliffs and snow!"

"You have a ready answer," said she and laughed; "below there is a charming meadow! There are my goats! I take good care of them! I lose none of them, what is mine, remains mine!"

"You are bold!" said Rudy.

"So are you!" answered she.

"Have you any milk? Do give me some, my thirst is intolerable!"

"I have something better than milk," said she, "and you shall have it! Travellers came yesterday with their guide, but they forgot a flask of wine, such as you have never tasted; they will not come for it, I shall not drink it, so drink you!"

She brought the wine, poured it in a wooden cup and handed it to Rudy.

"That is good," said he, "I have never drunk such a warming, such a fiery wine!" His eyes beamed, a life, a glow came over him; all sorrow and oppression seemed to die away; gushing, fresh human nature stirred itself within him.

"Why this is the schoolmaster's Annette," exclaimed he, "give me a kiss!"

"Yes, give me the beautiful ring, which you wear on your finger!"

"My engagement ring?"

"Just that one!" said the young girl and pouring wine into the cup, put it to his lips and he drank. Then the joy of life streamed in his blood; the whole world seemed to belong to him. "Why torment one's self? Every thing is made for our enjoyment and happiness! The stream of life is the stream of joy, and forgetfulness is felicity!" He looked at the young girl, it was Annette and then again not Annette; still less, an enchanted phantom, as he had named her, when he met her near Grindelwald. The girl on the mountain was fresh as the newly fallen snow, blooming as the alpine rose and light as a kid; and a human being like Rudy. He wound his arm about her, looked in her strange clear eyes, yes, only for a second—but was it spiritual life or was it death which flowed through him? Was he raised on high, or did he sink into the deep, murderous ice-pit, deeper and ever deeper? He saw icy walls like bluish green glass, numberless clefts yawned around, and the water sounded as it dropped, like a chime of bells; it was pearly, clear and shone in bluish white flames. The Ice-Maiden gave him a kiss, which made him shiver from head to foot and he gave a cry of pain. He staggered and fell; it grew dark before his eyes, but soon all became clear to him again; the evil powers had had their sport with him.

The alpine maiden had vanished, the mountain hut had vanished, the water beat against the bare rocky walls and all around him lay snow. Rudy wet to the skin, trembled from cold and his ring had disappeared, his engagement ring, which Babette had given him. He tried to fire off his rifle which lay near him in the snow but it missed. Humid clouds lay in the clefts like firm masses of snow and Vertigo watched for her powerless prey; beneath him in the deep chasm it sounded as if a block of the rock was rolling down and was endeavouring to crush and tear up all that met it in its fall.

In the mill sat Babette and wept; Rudy had not been there for six days; he who had been so wrong; he who must beg her forgiveness, because she loved him with her whole heart.

In the Miller's House

"What confusion!" said the parlour-cat to the kitchen-cat.

"Now all is wrong between Rudy and Babette. She sits and weeps and he thinks no longer on her, I suppose.

"I cannot bear it!" said the kitchen-cat.

"Nor I," said the parlour-cat, "but I shall not worry myself any longer about it! Babette can take the red-whiskered one for a dear one, but he has not been here either, since he tried to get on the roof!"

Within and without, the evil powers ruled, and Rudy knew this, and reflected upon what had taken place both around and within him, whilst upon the mountain. Were those faces, or was all a feverish dream? He had never known fever or sickness before. Whilst he condemned Babette, he also condemned himself. He thought of the wild, wicked feelings which had lately possessed him. Could he confess everything to Babette? Every thought, which in the hour of temptation might have become a reality? He had lost her ring and by this loss had she won him back. Could she confess to him? It seemed as if his heart would break when he thought of her; so many recollections passed through his soul. He saw her a lively, laughing, petulant child; many a loving word, which she had said to him in the fullness of her heart, shot like a sunbeam through his breast and soon all there was sunshine for Babette.

She must be able to confess to him and she should do so.

He came to the mill, he came to confession; and this commenced with a kiss, and ended with the fact that Rudy was the sinner; his great fault was, that he had doubted Babette's fidelity; yes, that was indeed atrocious in him! Such mistrust, such violence could bring them both into misfortune! Yes, most surely! Thereupon Babette preached him a little sermon, which much diverted her and became her charmingly; in one article Rudy was quite right; the god-mother's relation was a jackanapes! She should burn the book that he had given her, and not possess the slightest object which could remind her of him.

"Now it is all arranged," said the parlour-cat, "Rudy is here again, they understand each other and that is a great happiness!"

"Last night," said the kitchen-cat, "I heard the rats say that the greatest happiness was to eat tallow candles, and to have abundance of tainted meat. Now who must one believe, the rats or the lovers?"

"Neither of them," said the parlour-cat, "that is the surest way!"

The greatest happiness for Rudy and Babette was drawing near; they were awaiting, so they said, their happiest day, their wedding day.

But the wedding was not to be in the church of Bex, nor in the miller's house; the god-mother wished it to be solemnized near her, and the marriage ceremony was to take place in the beautiful little church of Montreux. The miller insisted that her desire should be fulfilled; he alone knew what the god-mother intended for the young couple; they were to receive a bridal present from her, which was well worth so slight a concession. The day was appointed. They were to leave for Villeneuve, in time to arrive at Montreux early in the morning, and so enable the god-mother's daughters to dress the bride.

"Then I suppose there will be a wedding here in the house, on the following day," said the parlour-cat, "otherwise, I would not give a single mew for the whole thing!"

"There will be a feast here," said the kitchen-cat, "the ducks are slain, the pigeons necks wrung, and a whole deer hangs on the wall. My teeth itch just with looking on! To-morrow the journey commences!"

Yes, to-morrow! Rudy and Babette sat together for the last time in the mill.

Without was the alpine glow; the evening bells pealed; the daughters of the Sun sang: "What is for the best will take place!"

The Visions of the Night

The sun had gone down; the clouds lowered themselves into the Rhone valley—between the high mountains; the wind blew from the south over the mountains—an African wind, a Föhn,—which tore the clouds asunder. When the wind had passed, all was still for an instant; the parted clouds hung in fantastic forms between the forest-grown mountains. Over the hastening Rhone, their shapes resembled sea-monsters of the primeval world, soaring eagles of the air and leaping frogs of the ditches—they seemed to sink into the rapid stream and to sail on the river, yet they still floated in the air. The stream carried away a pine tree, torn up by the roots; and the water sent whirlpools ahead; this was Vertigo, with her attendants, and they danced in circles on the foaming stream. The moon shone on the snow of the mountain-peaks; it lighted up the dark forest and the singular white clouds; the peasants of the mountain, saw through their window panes, the nightly apparitions and the spirits of the powers of nature, as they sailed before the Ice-Maiden. She came from her glacier castle, she sat in a frail bark, a felled fir-tree; the water of the glaciers carried her up the stream out to the main sea.

"The wedding guests are coming!" was whizzed and sung in the air and in the water.

Visions without and visions within!

Babette dreamt a wonderful dream.

It appeared to her, as though she was married to Rudy, and had been so for many years. He had gone chamois hunting and as she sat at home, the young Englishman with the golden whiskers was beside her; his eyes were fiery, his words seemed endowed with magical power; he reached her his hand and she was obliged to follow him.

They flew from home. Steadily downwards.

A weight lay upon her heart and it grew ever heavier. It was a sin against Rudy, a sin against God; suddenly she stood forsaken. Her clothes were torn by the thorns; her hair had grown grey; she looked up in her sorrow and she saw Rudy on the edge of the rock. She stretched her arms towards him, but she ventured neither to call, nor to implore him; but she soon saw that it was not he himself, only his hunting coat and hat, which were hanging on his alpine staff, as the hunters are accustomed to place them, in order to deceive the chamois! Babette moaned in boundless anguish:

"Ah! would that I had died on my wedding day, my happiest day! Oh! my heavenly Father! That would have been a mercy, a life's happiness! Then we would have obtained, the best, that could have happened to us! No one knows his future!" In her impious sorrow, she threw herself down the steep precipice. It seemed as if a string broke, and a sorrowful tone resounded.

Babette awoke—the dream was at an end and obliterated; but she knew that she had dreamt of something terrible, and of the young Englishman, whom she had neither seen, nor thought of, for many months. Was he perhaps in Montreux? Should she see him at her wedding? A slight shadow flitted over her delicate mouth, her brow contracted; but her smile soon returned; her eyes sparkled again; the sun shone so beautifully without, and to-morrow, yes to-morrow was her and Rudy's wedding day.

Rudy had already arrived, when she came down stairs, and they soon left for Villeneuve. They were so happy, the two, and the miller also; he laughed and was radiant with joy; he was a good father, an honest soul.

"Now we are the masters of the house!" said the parlour-cat.

Conclusion

It was not yet night, when the three joyous people reached Villeneuve and took their dinner. The miller seated himself in an arm-chair with his pipe and took a little nap. The betrothed went out of the town arm in arm, out on the carriage way, under the bush-grown rocks, to the deep bluish-green lake. Sombre Chillon, with its grey walls and heavy towers, mirrored itself in the clear water; but still nearer lay the little island, with its three acacias, and it looked like a bouquet on the lake.

"How charming it must be there!" said Babette; she felt again the greatest desire to visit it, and this wish could be immediately fulfilled; for a boat lay on the shore and the rope which fastened it, was easy to untie. As no one was visible, from whom they could ask permission, they took the boat without hesitation, for Rudy could row well. The oars skimmed like the fins of a fish, over the pliant water, which is so yielding and still so strong; which is all back to carry, but all mouth to engulph; which smiles—yes, is gentleness itself, and still awakens terror—and is so powerful in destroying. The rapid current soon brought the boat to the island; they stepped on land. There was just room enough for the two to dance.

Rudy swung Babette three times around, and then they seated themselves on the little bench, under the acacias, looked into each other's eyes, held each other by the hand, and everything around them shone in the splendour of the setting sun. The forests of fir-trees on the mountains became of a pinkish lilac aspect, the colour of blooming heath, and where the bare rocks were apparent, they glowed as if they were transparent. The clouds in the sky were radiant with a red glow; the whole lake was like a fresh flaming rose leaf. As the shadows arose to the snow-covered mountains of Savoy, they became dark blue, but the uppermost peak seemed like red lava and pointed out for a moment, the whole range of mountains, whose masses arose glowing from the bosom of the earth.

It seemed to Rudy and Babette, that they had never seen such an alpine glow. The snow-covered Dent-du-Midi, had a lustre like the full moon, when it rises to the horizon.

"So much beauty, so much happiness!" they both said.

"Earth can give me no more," said Rudy, "an evening hour like this is a whole life! How often have I felt as now, and thought that if everything should end suddenly, how happily have I lived! How blessed is this world! The day ended, a new one dawned and I felt that it was still more beautiful! How bountiful is our Lord, Babette!"

"I am so happy!" said she.

"Earth can give me no more!" exclaimed Rudy.

The evening bells resounded from the Savoy and Swiss mountains; the bluish-black Jura arose in golden splendour towards the west.

"God give you that which is most excellent and best, Rudy!" said Babette.

"He will do that," answered Rudy, "to-morrow I shall have it! To-morrow you will be entirely mine! Mine own, little, lovely wife!"

"The boat!" cried Babette at the same moment.

The boat, which was to convey them back, had broken loose and was sailing from the island.

"I will go for it!" said Rudy. He threw off his coat, drew off his boots, sprang in the lake and swam towards the boat.

The clear, bluish-grey water of the ice mountains, was cold and deep. Rudy gave but a single glance and it seemed as though he saw a gold ring, rolling, shining and sporting—he thought on his lost engagement ring—and the ring grew larger, widened into a sparkling circle and within it shone the clear glacier; all about yawned endless deep chasms; the water dropped and sounded like a chime of bells, and shone with bluish-white flames. He saw in a second, what we must say in many long words. Young hunters and young girls, men and women, who had once perished in the glacier, stood there living, with open eyes and smiling mouth; deep below them chimed from buried towns the peal of church bells; under the arches of the churches knelt the congregation; pieces of ice formed the organ pipes, and the mountain stream played the organ. On the clear transparent ground sat the Ice-Maiden; she raised herself towards Rudy, kissed his feet, and the coldness of death ran through his limbs and gave him an electric shock—ice and fire. He could not perceive the difference.

"Mine, mine!" sounded around him and within him.
"I kissed you, when you were young, kissed you on your

mouth! Now I kiss your feet, you are entirely mine!"

He vanished in the clear blue water.

Everything was still; the church bells stopped ringing; the last tones died away with the splendour of the red clouds.

"You are mine!" sounded in the deep. "You are mine!" sounded from on high, from the infinite.

How happy to fly from love to love, from earth to heaven!

A string broke, a cry of grief was heard, the icy kiss of death conquered; the prelude ended; so that the drama of life might commence, discord melted into harmony.—

Do you call this a sad story?

Poor Babette! For her it was a period of anguish.

The boat drifted farther and farther. No one on shore knew that the lovers were on the island. The evening darkened, the clouds lowered themselves; night came. She stood there, solitary, despairing, moaning. A flash of lightning passed over the Jura mountains, over Switzerland and over Savoy. From all sides flash upon flash of lightning, clap upon clap of thunder, which rolled continuously many minutes. At times the lightning was vivid as sunshine, and you could distinguish the grape vines; then all became black again in the dark night. The lightning formed knots, ties, zigzags, complicated figures; it struck in the lake, so that it lit it up on all sides; whilst the noise of the thunder was made louder by the echo. The boat was drawn on shore; all living objects sought shelter. Now the rain streamed down.

"Where can Rudy and Babette be in this frightful weather!" said the miller.

Babette sat with folded hands, with her head in her lap, mute with sorrow, with screaming and bewailing.

"In the deep water," said she to herself, "he is as far down as the glaciers!"

She remembered what Rudy had related to her of his mother's death, of his preservation, and how he was withdrawn death-like, from the clefts of the glacier. "The Ice-Maiden has him again!"

There was a flash of lightning, as dazzling as the sunlight on the white snow. Babette started up; at this instant, the sea rose like a glittering glacier; there stood the Ice-Maiden majestic, pale, blue, shining, and at her feet lay Rudy's corpse. "Mine!" said she, and then all around was fog and night and streaming water.

"Cruel!" moaned Babette, "why must he die, now that the day of our happiness approached. God! Enlighten my understanding! Enlighten my heart! I do not understand thy ways! Notwithstanding all thy omnipotence and wisdom, I still grope in the darkness."

God enlightened her heart. A thought like a ray of mercy, her last night's dream in all its vividness flashed through her; she remembered the words which she had spoken: "the wish for the best for herself and Rudy."

"Woe is me! Was that the sinful seed in my heart? Did my dream foretell my future life? Is all this misery for my salvation? Me, miserable one!"

Lamenting, sat she in the dark night. In the solemn

stillness, sounded Rudy's last words; the last ones he had uttered: "Earth has no more happiness to give me!" She had heard it in the fullness of her joy, she heard it again in all the depths of her sorrow.

———————

A couple of years have passed since then. The lake smiles, the coast smiles; the vine branches are filled with ripe grapes; the steamboats glide along with waving flags and the pleasure boats float over the watery mirror, with their two expanded sails like white butterflies. The railroad to Chillon is opened; it leads into the Rhone valley; strangers alight at every station; they arrive with their red covered guide books and read of remarkable sights which are to be seen. They visit Chillon, they stand upon the little island, with its three acacias—out on the lake—and they read in the book about the betrothed ones, who sailed over one evening in the year 1856;—of the death of the bridegroom, and: "it was not till the next morning, that the despairing shrieks of the bride were heard on the coast!"

The book does not tell, however, of Babette's quiet life with her father; not in the mill, where strangers now dwell, but in the beautiful house, near the railway station. There she looks from the window many an evening and gazes over the chestnut trees, upon the snow mountains, where Rudy once climbed. She sees in the evening hours the alpine glow—the children of the Sun encamp themselves above, and repeat the song of the wanderer, whose mantle the whirlwind tore off, and carried away: "it took the covering but not the man."

There is a rosy hue on the snow of the mountains; there is a rosy hue in every heart, where the thought dwells, that: "God always gives us that which is best for us!" but it is not always revealed to us, as it once happened to Babette in her dream.

Winter Sleep

By Elinor Wylie

When against earth a wooden heel
Clicks as loud as stone and steel,
When snow turns flour instead of flakes,
And frost bakes clay as fire bakes,
When the hard-bitten fields at last
Crack like iron flawed in the cast,
When the world is wicked and cross and old,
I long to be quit of the cruel cold.

Little birds like bubbles of glass
Fly to other Americas,
Birds as bright as sparkles of wine
Fly in the night to the Argentine,
Birds of azure and flame-birds go
To the tropical Gulf of Mexico:
They chase the sun, they follow the heat,
It is sweet in their bones, O sweet, sweet, sweet!
It's not with them that I'd love to be,
But under the roots of the balsam tree.

Just as the spiniest chestnut-burr
Is lined within with the finest fur,
So the stony-walled, snow-roofed house
Of every squirrel and mole and mouse
Is lined with thistledown, sea-gull's feather,
Velvet mullein-leaf, heaped together
With balsam and juniper, dry and curled,
Sweeter than anything else in the world.
O what a warm and darksome nest
Where the wildest things are hidden to rest!
It's there that I'd love to lie and sleep,
Soft, soft, soft, and deep, deep, deep!

Velvet Shoes

By Elinor Wylie

Let us walk in the white snow
   In a soundless space;
With footsteps quiet and slow,
   At a tranquil pace,
    Under veils of white lace.

I shall go shod in silk,
   And you in wool,
White as a white cow's milk,
   More beautiful
    Than the breast of a gull.

We shall walk through the still town
   In a windless peace;
We shall step upon white down,
   Upon silver fleece,
    Upon softer than these.

We shall walk in velvet shoes:
   Wherever we go
Silence will fall like dews
   On white silence below.
    We shall walk in the snow.

The Authors   Their Works

Hans Christian Andersen

The Danish storyteller whose fairy tales reshaped world folklore, Andersen wrote with a luminous blend of innocence, yearning, and symbolic depth.

Elinor Wylie

An American poet of the early twentieth century known for her jewel-like imagery and exquisitely crafted verse, Wylie captured nature's beauty with vivid clarity and fierce imagination.

Placed together, these works reveal the dual nature of winter and the human soul.

The Snow Queen originates from Scandinavia. *The Ice-Maiden* is a tale from the Alps. Their elements are the same: snow, ice, cold. And yet their themes diverge in striking ways.

Meanwhile, Wylie's winter poems sparkle and illuminate their visions as clear and sharp as frost among these tales of winter.

ISBN: 979-8-9990563-4-4

Modern Odyssey Books
www.modernodysseybooks.com

Curated and edited by Maria Glymph

MODERN ODYSSEY

www.ingramcontent.com/pod-product-compliance
Lightning Source LLC
Chambersburg PA
CBHW050416110726
47899CB00008B/2743